Sail Me Away Home

Ann
Clare
LeZotte

SCHOLASTIC PRESS / NEW YORK

Text copyright © 2023 by Ann Clare LeZotte
Jacket illustrations copyright © 2023 by Julie Morstad
All rights reserved. Published by Scholastic Press, an imprint of Scholastic Inc., *Publishers since 1920*. SCHOLASTIC, SCHOLASTIC PRESS, and associated logos are trademarks and/or registered trademarks of Scholastic Inc.

The publisher does not have any control over and does not assume any responsibility for author or third-party websites or their content.

No part of this publication may be reproduced, stored in a retrieval system, or transmitted in any form or by any means, electronic, mechanical, photocopying, recording, or otherwise, without written permission of the publisher. For information regarding permission, write to Scholastic Inc., Attention: Permissions Department, 557 Broadway, New York, NY 10012.

While inspired by real events and historical characters, this is a work of fiction and does not claim to be historically accurate or portray factual events or relationships. Please keep in mind that references to actual persons, living or dead, business establishments, events, or locales may not be factually accurate, but rather fictionalized by the author.

Library of Congress Cataloging-in-Publication Number: 2022044151

ISBN 978-1-338-74250-3
10 9 8 7 6 5 4 3 2 1   23 24 25 26 27
Printed in Italy   183
First edition, November 2023
Book design by Marijka Kostiw

WHEN I WAS YOUNG

I SEARCHED LIBRARY SHELVES

FOR STORIES ABOUT THE DEAF.

SIGNS OF OUR PAST AND WHAT

IT MEANT TO ME IN THE PRESENT.

FOR THOSE FOLLOWING

A SIMILAR JOURNEY—THIS

BOOK IS FOR YOU.

"In other times you wandered lost in the world . . .

Your joys and sorrows were locked in your hearts . . .

But now, what a change!

It has come to you because you have become a nation."

—CLAUDIUS FORESTIER,
DEAF FRENCHMAN

Part One

America

This journal is to be returned to the family

of Mary Elizabeth Lambert, Chilmark, Massachusetts,

to be retrieved at a later date.

Her whereabouts are currently unknown.

Chapter One

Honeybees are happily drowsing in blooms before returning to their hives. *A swarm of bees in June is worth a silver spoon.* We'll have stores of honey for winter. The plovers, with their orange beaks and black squiggles across their foreheads, are nesting contentedly on the beach.

Meanwhile I'm grounded, like a rusty anchor sunk in a seabed. Brightly colored fish swim quickly around it. An old humpback whale passes overhead. Looking down, the great beast admires the grappler's patience. The reliable metal is waiting for someone to haul it to the surface and take off full speed.

While the students practice their penmanship, some yawning or falling sideways in their seats, I shut my journal and wipe my brow. I rise and try to pry open a window painted shut in the Meeting House classroom. I'm careful not to cuss.

Townsfolk believe if I could manage a child rendered feral by abuse on the mainland, I am a good match for their offspring. Not all the school's teachers have been deaf but it's an advantage. Papa says my signing is most expressive.

Oh, I have tales to tell! But I'm relegated to the standard teachings dictated by our stuffy town council. If I had wind in my sails, I could push beyond them. I had such resolve when I last returned from the mainland, but without any new opportunities, it's dribbled away.

My encouraging mentor, Mrs. Pye, wasn't nearly as short-tempered as I am. I was her pupil in the traveling school that lands in Chilmark during the months when children unlace their boots and stare longingly out the windows.

They don't need me, I secretly think. I fold my skirt under me and sit at the desk. The students are mainly woolly-headed and meek like our sheep. They like to trick me but fortunately, not too often. No Wampanoag children are allowed here for learning, and I sneak in the three young Irish boys working at our farm when they show interest. I am determined to treat all—no matter their dress, parentage, or how many acres their family owns—as equal. But I long for a challenge, someone to reach and be inspired by, like Beatrice.

She was my first pupil, the girl locked on the top floor of a well-respected manor outside of Boston. When we first met, she was filthy and seemingly without language. She frightened me. It wasn't because I didn't realize the deaf outside of my village—where a high percentage are born without hearing—were treated monstrously. I did. But before I saw her as her own person and learned her history, I viewed her as what I might have become if I had been born anywhere but Martha's Vineyard. The most important thing she showed me is that we needn't be exactly alike, even in communication, to understand and support each other. I don't use oral speech as she does, but we have much in common.

For a moment, Beatrice's name seems to linger in the air, written in the dust the children produce by happily banging their erasers to clean them. I hope she's at home with the Mashpee Wampanoag Tribe on Cape Cod, not taken back to . . . *Stop fretting over what you cannot change!*

I'm broken from my reverie by movement in the classroom. The half dozen pupils all turn to look toward one of their own, puzzled.

Liam, a nephew of Papa's farmhand Eamon, is proving himself more observant than I first imagined. When he arrived with his brothers from County Galway, he would provoke me at every turn. He learned our island sign language easily as soon as he chose to, so quickly that I knew he'd been absorbing it all along.

He sits in the back and raises his arms to spell with both hands.

"Beltane," he signs. His dark eyes are mischievous.

Zounds! Just what the council warned me against. I imagine Reverend Lee shaking his head at the pulpit.

"May, last month," I sign, my hands turning back the invisible pages of a calendar. The other students look between us.

"No school before," he insists. "We celebrate now."

At the sign for "celebrate," the children put aside the slates I haven't yet checked and corrected. They jump up out of their boredom. I feel a stirring too. I'm sure Mrs. Pye would agree that it's the students who bring the lessons and an otherwise bare teaching space to life. Though I've been slack in my duties.

Can I teach what he's asking?

Chapter Two

I march ahead of the children. Swinging arms and broadening smiles, they're glad to be outdoors. It was a short spring, and the heat is coming on.

Is someone behind that white oak watching us? I catch a glimpse of a figure, who appears distorted, like looking through a drinking glass. When I startle, the students look at me oddly. I gather myself and move forward. Such visions—bloodred and hard to shake—are a regular occurrence lately. Luckily, nature gives me succor and often sweeps them away.

We walk under the shade of trees. Our path has not lately been trod but is safe from nettles and other stings. I turn back to clap, waving my hands over my head, and make sure they're all following.

We reach a field behind Mr. Butler's property. I can't remember if it has a name, but it's large enough to have celebrated May Day in times of old. In all my life, I've never seen a colorful pole here, with villagers dancing around it.

I begin my ancient history lesson. "During the Roman Republic, a festival was held every year. It was a celebration of the coming summer. The Latin poet Ovid reports goats and hares were released as part of the festivities."

"What sort of festivities?" Liam asks, smirking.

"Paganism," I sign grimly, determined to ruin his fun.

The other children look at one another with wide eyes and gaping mouths when I make the sign of a wild goat man. I have only ever used it with my childhood best friend, Nancy, never in polite society. It's made by indicating a beard with your fist on your chin, and then two fingers as horns on your forehead. It's best (or worst!) if you include a rude sneer.

They will likely tell their parents, but I can say it was a warning against activities opposed to the church's teachings.

That is, if Liam is content to let it go.

He stands back to give room for his storytelling. "Bonfires are lit in Ireland and cattle driven between them to protect them from disease."

I'm beguiled by this information. I'll add it to my written record of our town. But I must keep the promises I made.

"We don't speak of those things here," I reprimand him. "They are against God."

As if he were staring at those dancing flames, he continues, speaking without signing.

"Beannaich, a Thrianailt fhioir nach gann."

"What did he say?" I ask a girl named Caroline.

"I don't know, miss," she signs. "It's a language I've never heard."

Liam signs and speaks: "There is another god called Bel!"

At this, several children shriek and look much disturbed. Caroline takes my hand, and her younger sister, Kate, clutches my skirt.

I grab Liam's arm and shake him, signing with my other hand. "You little devil, you!"

He wriggles free and begins to dance skillfully on bent legs.

"Let's all be goats!" he signs. He twirls off in the field's waving grass.

I do the only thing a teacher can under the

circumstances. I laugh, clutching the stays at my side with one hand and slapping my knee with the other.

Even little Kate, who has tears in her eyes, smiles to see me so gay. Have I been such a scold lately?

Michael, a cousin of my former schoolmate Sarah Hillman, decides to follow Liam's example. He doesn't have the same grace or slyness, but he's expressing himself.

"I want to be a hare!" Caroline signs in a flurry. She jumps rabbitlike, straying farther from our path. Kate toddles behind, skipping as best she can.

I won't dizzy whoop among them. But my heart feels free, and I wait to gather them. Too long I wait. We are seen.

Chapter Three

"You behaved like a child," Mama signs. We are folding laundry in the kitchen.

"I have no one else to blame," I reply. "I took the children outside into the field. I guided the lesson."

"That's a fine admission for the town council. I am your mother."

"What shall I say?" I sign.

"Take me into your confidence, just once!"

"I have nothing to share."

I drop Mama's undergarments on the floor next to our herding dog, Sam, who followed me—covered in hay and clover—from the barn through the back door. Mama gives me a withering look.

Why am I being so petulant? "I'm sorry," I sign.

"I'm not asking you to be contrite," Mama signs.

"Then, what?"

"There you go," she signs. "Putting up that wall."

"What wall?" I inquire.

"The one you've built around you since your last

trip off-island," she signs sadly, resting on a chair. "The first time of course was not by choice. You were abducted to Boston by that deceiver Andrew Noble, who sought to make a name for himself by determining the cause of widespread deafness in Chilmark. To my shame, it happened right under our noses! But then you *chose* to become a tutor at the Vale and went on to Quincy and Cape Cod without so much as a word of discussion—"

I interrupt, so I don't have to relive all these memories.

"That wall—it's not on purpose," I sign, surprised to find myself engaging with her. "I know I seem shut off. I still love you and Papa and the farm, but . . ."

"What?" She shakes her hands in front of her, trying to grasp my meaning.

"To tell the truth," I sign, "I laughed for the first time in a long while when the children misbehaved."

Do I detect a small smile?

Mama tucks a loose hair back into her bun. "I shouldn't have scolded you. You've never done well under strict restraints. I want you to feel settled here like me, but I've begun to accept it's not in your nature."

Relief floods me, like a sparking tide rushing in when my feet are hot and dry on the sand. Could it be that Mama finally sees me for me?

"There's your gaiety," she says, gently pinching my cheek. "I am at a loss for how to help you, my daughter. I can only offer what you see around you. But I know it's not enough to fulfill your yearnings. Our Lord broke the mold, then fashioned a new one when He made you."

I move toward her, wanting to take her hands in mine.

"But every time you leave—despite all your passionate efforts—you come back hurt and troubled."

I drop my hands, and it feels like she recedes. I glimpse something out of the corner of my eye. A burning figure standing next to the hearth. It doesn't have eyes, but I feel I'm being watched.

"Don't look at her!" I must sign outside my mind because Mama looks alarmed.

"Who, Mary?"

Who was I warning? The apparition or me?

"This can't go on!" Mama stands and signs. The new intimacy—woven like gossamer between us—vanishes.

"If I let down my wall . . ." I sign.

"I can help!" Mama urges.

"I may cause harm," I reply.

Mama leans on the kitchen table Papa built. She wipes her eyelids. Is she thinking or crying? She looks up to sign.

"A greater course of action is needed. You will have to answer to the town council for your behavior choices with the students, but then you will ride with Reverend Lee to Tisbury. He needs to stop briefly at the parish there. You must be healed."

I could use his counsel and I'd like to see other sights. I want to rejoin the society of my good townsfolk. But I feel apart. Will I ever find something to grasp on to—a way to be of use that lies beyond all I know?

Chapter Four

Town council meetings rule on specific matters such as slandering neighbors or stealing fruit from another's orchard. Under the most serious circumstances, they may also censure townsfolk. In my youth, an old man who blasphemed in exaggerated signs to all who entered the church was forced to move to an isolated wilderness.

I shake off the memory as I stand outside the Meeting House with Papa, dressed in my best and holding my grandmother's Bible.

"Formality," Papa signs.

"I'm on trial," I sign. "I have gone against my schoolteacher duties and used a blasphemous sign, knowing it was wrong." I squeeze his hand to dispel the worry from his hazel eyes. I will have to stand alone, but I am glad to have him nearby, without judgment or disappointment. I feel safe with him like no other.

The doors open, and Nancy's father, Mr. Skiffe, steps out to greet us and lead us in. He is an abusive alcoholic who often spars with Papa over his progressive views. Last time I saw my friend, she was living in Quincy with her uncle Jeremiah to study music and be free from her father's cruel influence. I curtsy and try not to show my feelings.

Four men I have known my whole life have pushed Reverend Lee's lectern aside and set up five chairs in a row. My desk, filled with books and papers, is at the other end of the room. I sit on a wooden bench like one of my students. Papa stands between me and the council. The empty chair is his. Though neutral in town affairs, he's clearly on the side of my well-being. This may silently influence the others.

Mr. Skiffe signs first. "Mary Elizabeth Lambert, please rise."

I do as he says, my carriage erect and my gaze direct.

It's Mr. Butler's turn. "I saw the most alarming sight as I was surveying my property last Tuesday. Your students were frolicking in an unwholesome fashion, even the two girls, while you stood by amused. Can you confirm this?"

"I cannot confirm what you saw. I can only state my purpose in bringing the children there."

Out of the corner of my eye, I see Papa shift his weight and cross his arms. Although he and Mama gave advice on my defense, I must say what I believe to be true. Papa will jump in if I falter, which fortifies me.

Mr. Butler is visibly annoyed. He twists the ring on his little finger.

"And what was the purpose of you bringing the children there?" he signs.

"We were having an outdoor lesson," I reply plainly.

Mr. Pye, the most amiable of the group, interjects, "When my wife was the teacher, she too took her students on jaunts to learn about the natural world."

My heart lightens. He's giving me a line of defense. But I stay my course.

"I do remember Mrs. Pye's botany lessons fondly," I remark.

"Yes, yes," Mr. Skiffe sneers. "But what was your purpose *on that day*?"

"A Latin poem by Ovid describes a festival that took place in the Roman Republic this time of year, allegedly in a field like the one behind Mr. Butler's property."

Mr. Pye signs and speaks, "It's been some time

since I brushed up on my Latin, but I think I recall this poem."

Mr. Skiffe is relentless. "So by bringing the children to the field, you meant to reenact this ancient, ungodly festival?"

"No, sir!" I state defiantly.

Mr. Butler jumps in. "Explain to me what I saw, then."

"One of my pupils recalled hearing of the festival, which is sometimes called May Day—"

Mr. Skiffe interrupts. "Which pupil was it?"

"I can't recall," I state, crossing my fingers behind my back.

Old Mr. Tilton finally speaks. Mr. Pye translates for him. "You came in here carrying a family Bible, young lady."

"That is true. It belonged to my grandmother, and I read it daily."

The town elder is not satisfied. He quotes Proverbs 12:22: "'The Lord detests lying lips, but he delights in people who are trustworthy.'"

My fib is to protect a student. I consider it a vow of my profession and keep silent.

Mr. Butler is back at it. "A child reported that a language was recited, neither English nor Latin."

"I could not hear it," I reply.

Mr. Skiffe sneers at me. "Several children said you made a sign they had never seen before, which shocked and frightened them."

"On my honor, I was not promoting paganism."

The council looks at one another.

Mr. Butler signs, "You spelled that word on your hands. Please show us the sign you used with the children."

This is the one thing Mama implored me not to do. But I must appease the council.

"I will show you exactly as I signed it yesterday." I affect an impish countenance and make the sign of a wild goat man.

Does Mr. Skiffe clutch his breast? I can't imagine there's much that makes him blush.

Old Mr. Tilton speaks, with Mr. Pye again interpreting. "Where did you learn that obscenity?"

That question is easy to answer. "From my late friend Ezra Brewer."

Heads shake, but no one doubts it's true. Ezra

Brewer was a hoary sailor, and also a careful keeper of history on the island. He was so learned in our ways, including the bits he enjoyed most—the ones likely to get a rise out of respectable townsfolk.

"Why," the elder continues, "would you teach it to children under your care?"

If I am going to continue to protect Liam, I must step carefully here.

"That's a good question, sir," I sign with deference. "I never had any intention of doing so. Once I recalled the poem by Ovid, the children naturally had questions. As an educator, I feel students can add much—"

Mr. Skiffe interjects, "I hope you meant to frighten the young ones, to keep them from straying from God's path."

Mr. Butler signs, "They certainly strayed from the path, romping in the field behind my property."

"I should have stopped the frolicking," I admit. "It seemed like good-natured fun."

Mr. Pye signs, "I think a verbal warning is an appropriate punishment. Miss Lambert is considered a capable teacher, and this is her first offense."

Mr. Skiffe asserts, "It's not quite as simple as that. One of the fathers is pulling his child from the school. He feels the lad has been corrupted."

I imagine it's Michael Hillman, the first to dance with Liam. The little rat! I hold my tongue and my breath.

Mr. Butler signs, "We're unlikely to find another teacher for the season. If we remove any teaching of Ovid and outdoor lessons, and Mary apologizes at the town meeting, I could agree to the verbal warning—with no guarantee that Mary returns to the position next summer."

I glance at Papa for support but cannot keep my hands still. "Why are we condemning a Roman poet? How will I keep the children indoors through August?"

Old Mr. Tilton says, "You'll manage."

I twist my hands, searching for the right words to express my concern.

They take my silence as agreement. Papa also feels it's over. I sense his relief. He walks toward me with an arm extended.

Mr. Skiffe stands. "One more thing. We know it was that bogtrotter who led the lesson astray. He and his kind are permanently banned from attending our school!"

"His *kind*?" I lunge forward in protest, but I'm overlooked.

Mr. Skiffe points to Papa. "Keep them working in your fields where they belong. They have no need for an education. Their language and traditions are corrupting."

I'm aghast and feel censured even though I'm keeping my position.

Without comment, Papa gently takes my arm and leads me out into the sunshine.

"I will talk to Eamon," he signs. "If you have time, you can continue Liam's lessons in the privacy of our barn. You do best you can."

Riding home in the cart, I sob. Papa hands me the cloth he uses to wipe his brow. It's unusual for me to display such emotion. But first Beatrice. Now Liam. Both ostracized simply for living among those who judge others but don't hold up a mirror to their own bigotry. I refuse to believe any child is less worthy than another and shouldn't be educated.

Chapter Five

Taking a journey with Reverend Lee in his two-wheeled horse trap is invigorating! It's quicker than our oxcart, and he knows the route from Chilmark to West Tisbury well. There's enough distance to cross (five miles on the map) that I have time for thought and observation.

I see a surfeit of striped skunks with small, pointed heads walk regally by the side of the road. Their plumed tails sway, cocked and ready to fire. They must be returning to their den. I've heard their babies are born deaf and blind.

I start to relax as we travel beyond our high road, and familiar scenes crop up all around. I jot down some notes in my journal—an episode in my history. Our neighboring town, Tisbury, is mostly low-lying and at sea level. Its outwash plains, made of sand and gravel carried by running water from melting glacial ice, are so old, only the Wampanoag know their whole story.

It was a rare expedition when Papa took me and my brother, George, to the Tisbury docks. While my horizons have expanded with trips to the mainland and the Cape, the Vineyard will always remain in my blood even as I long for further exploration.

I see smatterings of daisies among the pine and scrub oak. The pink-and-green hydrangeas make me breathe a bit deeper. Mixed with salt air, it's a scent I'm sure can't be found anywhere else.

Reverend Lee slows the carriage so we can have a small picnic. Mama packed bread, cheese, and cold meat. My host drinks ale, and I take the stopper off a milk bottle.

"I'm sure you heard about the town council meeting," I sign.

"Naturally," he signs. "I don't take it seriously. Children have curious minds. And if we are to live together, it's necessary to understand we don't all share the same customs and beliefs."

"Explain that to the council," I tease with one hand while raising my bottle of milk.

"It will take time, maybe generations, for changes to occur."

"What do we do in the meantime?" I ask with urgency.

"Just as you are," he signs.

"I wish to do more," I sign.

When I returned from being kidnapped by Andrew Noble, Mrs. Pye told me a story she'd heard from her sailor brother-in-law, Daniel Trees. During his travels, he visited a school for the deaf in Paris. He was taken aback to find so many deaf people walking together and signing confidently like our Chilmark neighbors. I remember going to bed, dreaming of such a school in America, with me as a teacher. Could that be my future?

"It's obvious you're stalled here," he observes.

"Mama and Papa don't see that!"

"I'm certain they do. You are strong-willed and passionate. They know they cannot hold you here much longer, but they fear for your safety."

"I don't think I—"

"Can you honestly say you haven't put yourself in harm's way?" he interrupts.

"I suppose not," I sign, grasping my fist in front of my face. "I thought Mama was beginning to accept my different ways. Papa misses me, but I suspect I'm fulfilling his dreams by going off on adventures."

"I believe you have a mission, Mary. But you mustn't be careless. Heed my words."

"I will try," I sign.

Reverend Lee packs up the remnants of our meal before I can ask him what he sees in my future. Something in his manner seems veiled. I didn't inquire if he had a specific purpose in bringing me here. Mama was under the impression it was simply for moral instruction and to clear my mind by traveling outside Chilmark.

We continue at a quick pace. We're obviously expected someplace. I'm both amused and curious. Is Reverend Lee more of a slyboots than I imagined? Does he have a solution to my problems?

"Lambert's Cove! Named for my great-grandfather, the first recorded deaf Vineyarder. It isn't far from here!" I sign. Could this be our destination?

"I haven't forgotten it," Reverend Lee signs. "And we can pay a visit. But first, let me introduce you to some friends."

"I'm happy to meet your friends," I sign, watching

him curiously. He appears nervous, which undermines his sneakiness. I narrow my eyes. Butterflies flutter in my stomach. I feel an old excitement begin to return.

"Indeed, they are very eager to meet you!"

The sun is going down, spreading colors in the sky like a painter's palette. The evening primrose starts to open its little yellow skirts. All of nature is going through its motions, and we can only gape, amazed.

Reverend Lee is uncommonly quiet as we drive on. It's a good thing I trust him. What activity could he have arranged for my benefit?

Chapter Six

We stop in front of a parsonage. Dating from 1688, it's believed to be the second-oldest home on the island, built by Josiah Standish, son of *Mayflower* passenger Captain Myles Standish. A fine design with pointed roofs and three chimneys, it sits on three acres abutting a sheep farm.

I note other carriages gathered in the road and wonder at the occasion. It is not the Sabbath, and I have had enough town meetings to last quite awhile. Please don't let it be a visiting preacher with too much to say.

Reverend Lee puts his hand on my shoulder as we approach the front door. What *is* he planning?

We are let into a dim entrance where a flock of parishioners fold their hands silently and flap their mouths like fish out of water. If they were told I was coming, they make no attempt to accommodate my deafness.

Reverend Lee pats his chest to invite me to be calm

though my blood is rising. This is the reason Papa rarely leaves Chilmark.

We enter a handsome large parlor, with enough space for fifteen of us to sit in rows. A cleric stands at the front with no interpreter beside him. Reverend Lee and I sit facing him. Why have I been brought here?

This meeting, whatever its purpose, is poorly planned! How shall I understand? It's unlike my friend and family counselor to put me at such a disadvantage.

The man leading the meeting sweeps his arms dramatically in all directions before speaking. I hope this is his custom and not for my benefit. I have met some on the Vineyard without deaf kin or fluency in our signs who use rudimentary hand signals and act awkwardly in our presence.

I look at Reverend Lee and shake my hands, asking, "What?"

The leader gestures to us as he speaks. Reverend Lee signs, "Follow me."

"No!" I sign. "I demand to know the meaning of all this."

"You will," he signs.

I'm suddenly aware of how closely our common exchange is being observed. A part of me feels like I'm back in the Boston doctor's examination room with Andrew Noble—a live specimen in an experiment controlled by outsiders.

Reverend Lee urges me forward. I can only guess it's because he worries I may not go along with his plan, whatever it is. What will be expected of me next? Why wasn't I told in advance?

The leader shakes his hand and pats me on the head like a small child.

I can't keep calm as Reverend Lee has asked. I turn to him and sign with distress. "You are betraying all you know about me. I feel stupid, embarrassed."

"Mary," he signs with shaking hands, "they are interested in your signs. Why don't you tell them a short story?"

"A story?" I stretch my hands like a spider weaves a web.

"Like the ones you used to sign to yourself when you walked up and down the high road as a girl."

Oh, I have many in mind and will make my mood known to this inhospitable, gaping crowd!

Reverend Lee looks deeply into my eyes while his hands move awkwardly. "I'm sorry . . . I . . . deceived you . . . and, well, your mother. But this is a rare opportunity for you to cross the Atlantic Ocean."

My heart drops to my knees, which almost buckle. What can be his meaning? Will my performance determine if I am offered passage to England or France? Might I be given a chance to visit the Paris school that Daniel Trees spoke of?

Reverend Lee nods as if reading my mind. "For all that you know, make sure it's holy. I will be the speaking voice."

I look at the faces fixed on me with curiosity. Most seem to be around Mama's age. The eldest appears to be the leader, and her face is sour as a bucket of lemons. Despite their differences, their countenance and demeanor are surprisingly similar. You can tell this group belongs together.

Only one has a face that shines with an inquisitive light. She has bright eyes and corn-silk hair wrapped around her head in a braid. The way she watches me is almost unnerving.

I take a deep breath. I don't know what this is about, but Reverend Lee has never put me on the wrong course before.

I create a sort of stage by walking back and forth in the space where I'll be performing. I rub my hands together and massage my arms up to my elbows—an echo of my wily mentor, the mesmerizing storyteller Ezra Brewer. I don't meet the eyes of the audience till I'm ready.

A lighthouse. Moon. Fisherman. He sets lobster traps. Clouds roll in.

Boat docking. Can't see clear. Fisherman turn back crouching. He can't hear.

HIT! Man down. Clouds pass. Moon shine bright. Other seamen carry body.

Lay out in worn clothes, clean, brushed. Brother comes to claim him. Never thought much of Fisherman. Rest of family hearing, respectable. Friends gather round. All deaf. Sing songs in signs. Like ocean calling him home. Brother amazed. Fisherman was loved by community not family. Brother cries silent.

I look up to faces sobbing. Did they understand the message of my story? Who did they pity, the fisherman or his brother?

Chapter Seven

Reverend Lee's expression tells me I performed well. The worshippers want a closer look at me. Sometimes when people gather around, it feels like an embrace. It can also be suffocating. They are hesitant to shake my hand or try to directly communicate with me.

The woman with the corn-silk braid steps forward. She wears a heavy woolen cape and her face is lit from within. Her polite smile leans naturally to one side, like an amiable smirk. She has dark blue eyes, the color of the sea, framed with yellow lashes. There is something almost hypnotic about her presence.

"Mary," Reverend Lee signs, "this is Miss Mitchell. She wants to express her gratitude to you for coming here today and sharing your story in sign language."

I curtsy to the lady. She smiles gently and nods. I look into her lively eyes, glad she didn't use oral speech with me.

She keeps her eyes on me as Reverend Lee attempts to interpret her words.

"Dear Mary," she says, "I am a part of something extraordinary. The Second Great Awakening is a Protestant religious revival that began in about 1795. Meetings are being held in small towns and large cities throughout the country. Our mission is soul winning, drawing Man back to his Maker."

It's likely she rehearsed her speech—but it feels like she's speaking just to me. She seems tender but not demonstrative, formidable but not overbearing. Her passion is evident. Though I can't see my role in it.

Miss Mitchell says, "I and several other young women joined a new organization called the American League of Commissioners for Foreign Missions. Have you heard of it?"

By this point, my chaperone is exhausted and out of his depth as an interpreter, so I retrieve my writing supplies from the carriage. Miss Mitchell and I continue to converse.

I have not heard of it, I write. *What is your purpose?*

Reverend Lee hovers behind my chair, looking over my shoulder.

We are interested in social reform. I recently came here from Tennessee, where we were spreading the word.

Thank you for explaining, I write. *I don't exactly understand it or how it applies to me.*

Let me tell you more, she writes with eagerness. *I have been invited to join several others on a voyage to the Middle East and Asia.*

That's very far away, I observe.

We go where we are needed under the guidance of Our Lord.

I'm starting to feel discouraged about Reverend Lee's promise of England and France.

I am blunt. *I wish you safe travels, but I'm not sure how this concerns me or why I was brought here today.*

I glance back at Reverend Lee, who speaks to Miss Mitchell.

She focuses her captivating eyes on me and writes, *We have heard of the deaf who are intelligent and communicate a full range of ideas and emotions through a hand language. I must say, I couldn't quite believe it until I saw your remarkable performance.*

I write directly, as if she's not a stranger. *There are many who consider sign language to be an inferior means of communication.*

Mary, have you have heard of Friar Melchor de

Yebra? He was a sixteenth-century monk. He made drawings of handshapes that represent the Spanish alphabet. I've been fascinated by the subject since my American League instructor related his story to me.

I sigh deeply. Miss Mitchell's fervor about sign languages could lead down a dangerous path. I've seen some who've learned two dozen signs begin to falsely instruct others. If they have a purely academic interest, separate from respecting the deaf who created it, there is no true engagement with our communities. I also resent that she knows something I don't about the history of signs! Could there be a hand alphabet that old?

Miss Mitchell jumps back in, eager not to lose my interest.

Can you imagine how Melchor de Yebra's brotherhood used the signs?

I suppose it could be useful to those who take a vow of silence.

Very clever! she replies. *He was also concerned for those who had lost speech to illness and could not make an intelligible confession to Our Lord.*

It's a charming story. I don't have the patience to

explain that sign language isn't a replacement for oral speech. While it can be useful to all people, it's a whole language—which reflects our unique way of thinking. A true understanding requires immersion with native signers. Perhaps she misspoke. I'm likely the first competent deaf person she's met. My eyes drift toward the door.

Miss Mitchell seizes my attention again.

Reverend Lee knows the parson here and thought you might like to join us, at least as far as the schools for the deaf and dumb in England and France.

Of course my curiosity is piqued. My ancestors are from England. And Paris?! The school Daniel Trees visited! *Do you intend to visit there?*

We believe exposure to the teaching methods would aid us in our ministries. There are so many suffering in the absence of the light of God. Due to their infirmities, they have never been brought to grace in a chapel. We must reach them too.

I don't like the sound of that. I can't tell if her religion is akin to Andrew Noble's science. George would remind me that in all disciplines, there's careful, intelligent study and research. But also fanaticism—a strong mind fixated on a single point, unable to adapt to outside influences.

I point to myself, asking my role in her grand missionary scheme. She senses my meaning, which gives me confidence.

You could help us gain entrance to these institutions, which Reverend Lee said would be of interest to you. He mentioned you are a fledgling teacher and interested in helping pitiable creatures.

Reverend Lee puts his hands gently on my shoulders. He is steadying me and I'm sure urging caution.

I surprise myself by simply writing, *I will think it over.*

Miss Mitchell stands when I do and clasps my hands. There could be a bond, even friendship between us—if she's sincere.

"Two weeks," she says with Reverend Lee interpreting again. That's how much time I have to decide. "I will be hoping and praying you'll choose to join us." She winks, with that sideways smile.

All seems well, but the altarpiece looks to be aflame. I'm burning too.

My chaperone must realize I've reached my limit.

He places hands together in prayer, expresses niceties, and moves us toward the exit.

"Is this invitation really possible?" I ask him after we drive awhile and make another stop.

He nods thoughtfully.

"Have you considered what my parents will say?"

"It's a Christian mission that will pass safely through political strife and look after your needs."

I side-eye him. As if it were that simple.

"Now you will directly answer my questions," I sign. "Being evasive doesn't suit you."

"I'm more comfortable being out in the open. I'm truly sorry if I compromised your dignity. I sometimes forget you can't hear."

I wince. It's not the compliment many may think.

He wrings his hands, knowing he's stumbled more than once.

"Don't forget again," I sign. "In Chilmark, deaf and hearing work together and care for one another—but it's different outside, even sometimes on the island."

He nods in recognition.

I sign, "Now tell me why Miss Mitchell's group was in Tennessee."

Reverend Lee rubs the knuckles on his long hands, which have become arthritic.

"The league is acquiring acres of land on South Chickamauga Creek. A mission will be built there to teach skills and provide a basic Christian education to Cherokee children."

"And you expect me to join them?" I sign, agitated. "I know you supported early Christian missionaries forcibly converting the Wampanoag to Praying Indians on our island. But you've come to feel it's best to let them believe and practice as they like."

"That is true," he replies.

"And now Indian children will be taken away to a mission school?"

"Mary, it's in your nature to try to do right by all. By traveling with the league, you will have opportunities to further your own interests while helping people. The steps you take may feel like a betrayal to others. Even people you care for. That happens to all of us as we grow. We inadvertently injure even those we love in the process of advancing our own ambitions."

I'll have to decide if I believe this.

"I won't go, then!"

"I've learned from mentors without always agreeing with them. And remember, religious travelers, those spreading the Word, can bring light to dark places!"

"The missionary league?"

"You have some similarities of purpose in aiding the deaf, and your deafness will keep you from their constant indoctrination!" His smile shows slight amusement.

I won't relent. "No! It's out of the question."

"Then you will not visit the deaf schools in England and Paris. I have worked to make the connections and offer you this chance. It will not come again."

I know he's right, and it would be childish to pretend I can accept with a clear conscience or stay home and be content. I heed his words but intend to seek another point of view. I don't tell him that I found Miss Mitchell entrancing, and I'm flattered she's interested in me and in sign language. Will I be able to push her away when it's time?

"You might as well air any other concerns," he signs.

"They will try to get me to the Middle East and Asia with them."

"They have given me their word they won't, Mary."

"Visiting the Paris school is the biggest incentive to agree to their terms. How will I get home if I go there?"

"One member of the party has promised to return with you."

I meet his eyes. "Why do they really want me?"

His smile is rueful. "You're . . . inspirational."

"Don't say it!"

"Let's put these discussions aside till we return to Chilmark."

"That's fine," I sign. "I should thank you for arranging the opportunity—whether or not I accept—though you could have been more forthcoming."

"Look where we are, Mary."

I hadn't noticed we've stopped at Lambert's Cove! Finally, something that makes sense: communing with the spirits of my ancestors and digging my toes into the white sand beach. My past began here—perhaps I will receive a signal for what lies ahead.

Chapter Eight

Somehow this hilly terrain escaped becoming the flatland that characterizes most of our island. I scale it, on hands and knees, like an obstinate ant. The rocks are slippery from moss and sea spray. I remove my shoes and stockings so my feet can grip them better. My skirt grows wet and heavy, but I persist. Climbing takes my mind from pretty Miss Mitchell and her questionable mission.

Atop the cliff, I hold my hand over my eyes to block the sun and spy Aquinnah in the distance. I've only been there with Papa a few times. Once we brought a spring lamb to my Wampanoag friend Sally and her late mother, Helen, while Sally's father, Thomas, was away working on a dangerous whaling ship.

Sally took my hand and we walked close to the edge of the cliffs. I have never seen the like: Layers of sand, gravel, and clay of various hues created a mile-long rainbow. Erosion turned the sea a red color. I'm too far from that spot to see it clearly now.

I run down a sand dune, holding my boots in my hands. The sand is soft and warm between my toes. I walk along the shore, observing the sea. I no longer see lions leaping out of the surf as in my childhood imagination. Today, the ocean seems full of faces, watching me watching them. Is it an ancestral gathering? Do my forebearers look to me to show them their future? Two gray eyes and a watery mouth slip under the waves. It must be old Jonathan Lambert keeping watch over his cove!

I glance back at Reverend Lee, waving his hand over his head to call me back to the carriage. I wave back, but don't retreat.

I stand among dried black seaweed with hard balls I like to burst. I feel I've been beckoned here to ask a question of my relatives whose breath is now sea air.

I stretch out my arms rigidly in front of me. I press my palms together at a point. I twirl, twirl, twirl, almost throwing myself in broad circles.

Seagulls follow my pattern overhead.

My hair is unloosed from its bun. It covers my eyes like a blindfold.

I stop when the wind is knocked out of me.

The compass needle I've become points northeast.

Is my next step truly to visit our ancestral home—England? Somehow, it seems inevitable. Even with Reverend Lee's direction, I can't believe this chance has randomly arisen.

There could be other interpretations. Am I trying to convince myself? I'm disgusted by the league's actions with the Cherokee and uncertain they'll be better with the deaf. My thoughts spin in the salt air as I run back to Reverend Lee.

On the ride home, my stockings and boots are filled with scratchy sand. I can barely keep my eyes open as my chaperone indicates the old cranberry bog. From a distance, it looks like a cerulean pool filled with scarlet flowers. He points out the oak and beech trees, unlike our scrub oaks and pines. The sights seem to blur and blend till I fall into a slumber.

I awake with a jolt at the gate to my home. Mama, who is gathering a pitcher of water from the well, walks toward us, smiling.

Reverend Lee pinches my leg. I almost yelp, but I know he is cautioning me not to blurt out everything about Miss Mitchell and my performance at the parsonage. Why is he being my confederate when he usually tells all to my parents? Does he still feel guilty about bringing Andrew Noble to the island and not recognizing the warning signs?

After I climb down from the cart, I reach my hand into my pocket. Mama is delighted to see red and blue sea glass to add to her collection.

We say goodbye to my chaperone. Mama wraps her shawl around my shoulders, and I carry the pitcher to the house for her.

Behind us the sky is darkening. It may be rain or something else. I feel a strange shiver run along my spine, as if a spectral finger touches me. I shouldn't glance back but I do. Just as Reverend Lee takes up the reins to depart, I think I see fiery embers in the eyes of his horse. Hellfire streams from its nostrils in great bursts. I gasp.

Mama turns to see what I see, then looks at me worriedly. She tightens her shawl around our shoulders and rushes me into our front parlor as passersby take notice.

Why am I plagued by these terrifying visions? And what could they mean?

Chapter Nine

After I brush my gown and wash my face, I join Mama and Papa in the kitchen for supper. The smell of beef stew and fresh-baked muffins makes my mouth water and my stomach gurgle. I'm full of mixed emotions. The missionary meeting and Miss Mitchell's invitation have left me feeling nervy, raw. I'm not yet ready to consider how much of my integrity I'll compromise to get what I want, but the question is tickling the back of my mind.

Papa signs grace and we silently enjoy our family feast. My parents sit at either end of the rectangular table and I on the north side. Four sides minus one. George's presence is always felt. It's difficult to fathom it's been almost six years since the horrible carriage accident that claimed him. I still wish I hadn't witnessed it. Sometimes I imagine him bursting in upon us, full of dreams and ideas. His light seemed inextinguishable. It comforts me to visit his grave and leave seeds, fossils, and other items that would interest him.

Now it is down to me. To carry the family name. Make my mark in the world. Help Mama and Papa when they grow old.

Why can't I be content with those aspirations? Why must I always be planning the next adventure? I want to fulfill my obligations, but other tides flow inside me.

"That woman has written to you again," Mama signs. "I thought that was all finished after you returned home last time."

"Which woman?" I ask.

"The one who aided you in Boston, then invited you to become a tutor at the manor house in Waltham. Miss Nora O'Neal," she spells with her hands.

"What did it say?"

"I didn't open it, Mary. I'll give it to you when the dishes are washed and put away."

I'm full of curiosity. But mostly relief. The last time I saw Nora she had just hit Mr. Norwich, the odious butler at the Vale, with a flatiron. She was helping me and Beatrice escape with Nancy's aid.

I've lost my appetite from excitement, but I don't rush eating or push my plate aside.

Where could Nora be? What could she do if she left two employers without references, even if she was morally correct? One tried to take advantage of her while the other called for her complicity in keeping an innocent girl captive.

Papa must see the color rising in my cheeks. He pats my hand gently. Mama stares straight ahead as she lifts the fork to her mouth. The good humor with which she greeted me is gone. The last time I received a letter from Nora, it drew me to the Vale. They must be worrying that she'll entice me into another dangerous adventure. What else could she possibly want?

I glance at the large brick hearth. Is it the source of my waking nightmares? Do the cinders fly up the chimney to form the apparitions revealed only to me, then quickly disappear?

No, I've always associated the source of our home's warmth with affection, like another mother. I was rocked by the hearth as a baby. I feed my poor writing to its flames, and it keeps my failures secret.

"Mary." Mama is behind me now, cradling her cheek in her palm to make my sign name. I read strain and fear on her face, and she hasn't even learned about the missionaries yet. She points at my dish. Time to clean up!

After everything is put away, I retreat to my room with the letter.

The envelope is wrinkled and smeared with several people's handwriting. I wonder if it went astray. I kiss it to wish for good news, then open it carefully.

Dear Mary,

I pray this letter arrives safely as I gave it to a sailor I didn't know. Let me catch you up on my doings. I think you'll be interested.

Life goes on as normal (if you can call it that) at the Vale. I left quickly after you and Beatrice. Ben and I rode away to safety, but he returned to resume his duties as groundskeeper.

Mr. Norwich is on the run. The family intends to send the traitor to the gallows if they see hide or hair of him.

Mrs. Collins and Ellie stayed on, though the girl holds her head a little higher due to your influence.

I can only live with my sister and take in laundry for so

long. I'm hesitant to ask, but is it at all possible I could visit your island to become more acquainted with the sign language? (I have tried to keep practicing on my own.) That is, if your townsfolk will welcome me.

I send you my very best wishes.

Sincerely,
Miss Nora O'Neal

I put the letter under a piece of petrified wood on my desk and pace the room. When I fear I'll wear out the braided rug, I return to the kitchen, looking for company.

Mama sits by the fire with her needlepoint neglected in her lap as she gazes unseeing into the flames. She looks up, squaring her shoulders, at the sound of my bedroom door closing gently behind me. I see desperate hope and a dash of fear in her eyes before she can compose herself. She picks up her needlepoint and pretends she has been working on it the whole time.

"News?" she asks.

I hesitate as worry momentarily clouds her countenance.

"None of Beatrice," I answer, because she is most important to me.

"Surely that must be good," notes Mama, "if she does not tell you she's been returned to the Vale."

I nod. She is right. But it would give me peace in my heart to know she is well, not just that her absence is promising. "Nora—" I begin, and I see Mama brace herself. "She wants to come to Martha's Vineyard. To stay," I clarify.

Mama looks as if you could knock her over with a feather! It's clear of all the thoughts she was having, this was not one of them. "Oh." I see her mouth form the word. "Well . . . if there was room on this island for Andrew Noble, I'm certain someone will be able to house Miss Nora O'Neal."

"I thought . . ." I pause.

Am I certain of what I am about to say? Do I mention it now when I have not given it the reflection I'd intended?

"Perhaps she could stay here, in my room, while I am away."

Mama goes stiff and sets her needlepoint aside carefully, deliberately. "You intend to leave again?" she says, and I see her shoulders rise and fall with a sigh.

I take a seat across from her and cradle her hand gently. "I have not yet decided. Reverend Lee introduced me to a group of missionaries who would provide safe travel for me to the Continent. Mrs. Pye mentioned a large school for the deaf in Paris. Imagine!"

"That far!" she signs, her brow furrowed. "Reverend Lee has not spoken to me about this, not in specifics. Though he has counseled me, as he always does. I can see it myself, that you feel trapped."

"Not trapped!" I object, but I work my fingers, trying to think of a word to describe the frustration I've felt of late.

"Restrained, then," Mama says. "Mary, you pranced like a wild goat in a field."

A smile breaks through me, and I can't help but chuckle. Mama joins me. "To teach a lesson!" I tell her with exaggerated piety as she shakes her head with a grin. "And I did not join the children's game. How stories grow!"

"Europe," Mama signs, spreading out an invisible map with palaces and soldiers in front of her. "It's not possible."

"I do not know if this is the right path," I tell her. I don't want to admit that I'm conflicted. I must appear resolute. "Would you give me your blessing?"

She is quiet for a moment, putting her cheek in her hand as she watches the fire dance and pop. "I have never wanted you to leave," she says slowly. "You may tell Miss O'Neal that we'll welcome her, but you ask too much of me. I will never consent to send you across the globe."

I look away from her in despair. The window over the sink suddenly catches my eye.

"There's a fire outside!" I sign, moving my hands like flames rising.

Sensibly, Mama pours water from the pitcher into a bucket, and we rush out.

The evening is dim. Stars are starting to appear but not in full glimmer. No fire roars. No tree is scorched to the roots. It was a false alarm.

Mama drops the bucket and seizes me by the shoulders. She searches my confused eyes, which look through her. Letting go, she raises her trembling hands.

"What is it?" she signs in a whisper. "Tell me what you're seeing."

"I cannot tell you because I do not know," I admit. "But these visions seem as real as you or me."

Mama looks stricken.

"Come indoors now, Mary. People are talking. I'll make you a cup of tea and put you to bed. You may need to be baptized again."

"What?" I demand. "I am in full possession of my faculties, except for brief moments. I'm trying to discern the origin of these episodes. What people are you talking about?"

In my room, Mama rocks me in her arms. I am too big and feel ungainly. But the rhythm is soothing her, so I don't object. I can feel her murmuring while I'm pressed against her chest.

There's no doubt I must leave. Something can be found to make me whole again. But not here—I feel urged forward as if blown by a gale. Reverend Lee knows this. How can I convince my parents?

Chapter Ten

Even though it's the Sabbath, I don't want to wear my best hat. Why would I if I'm to be dunked in holy water like when I was a baby? I ask Papa if Mama really expects it, and he shakes his head in uncertainty. I share the feeling.

Mama is a practical person. We were laughing together last night until I brought up the missionary work. Is this her attempt to deny me the opportunity to travel, since it would take me months or a year to return home?

Our ox is moving slower than usual, as if he thinks we're taking him to auction. I fear it will be me on the block, and in my home chapel, no less. I hope Reverend Lee has prepared a hummer of a sermon—to avoid hard feelings from the town council meeting and delay a possible baptism. By the time we arrive, Mr. Pye is banging the gavel to mark the end of the town meeting.

It is uncommon for us to miss the weekly

gathering. All eyes are on us as we take our seats in a middle pew. If Nancy were here and saw my nervous expression, she'd likely stick out her tongue or cross her eyes. The thought makes me feel lighter.

Mr. Butler looks back at us, then turns to sign to his wife. He moves his hands in his lap. A private complaint or jest.

I look at Papa, who seems unshaken. It gives me some strength as Mama clasps my hands. Is she showing support or trying to prevent me from answering rebukes should there be any?

My old classmate Sarah Hillman will interpret at the pulpit. Her signing is more than adequate but will have none of the wit and color that Ezra Brewer brought to the task.

Though I've sat in this very meeting house all my life, it feels unfamiliar. I'm counting on Reverend Lee to bring me back into the circle.

"Neighbors," he begins, "how many of us have not sinned? Yet we often sit in judgment over others for actions that were negligible at worst."

I notice I'm vigorously nodding when Papa gently bumps me with his boot.

"Our Lord gives grace," Reverend Lee continues. "He asks us to forgive what may easily be forgiven, even if we find ourselves in doubt or misunderstanding of another's actions."

I feel soothed until I catch sight of Mr. Skiffe's twisted, purple face.

Reverend Lee goes on, with Sarah adding too many flourishes of her own to his simple sermon.

"It is part of our nature to create conflict, even to look for disagreement with those closest to us. If we are malcontent, we must pray for calm and understanding. To spread harsh speech and feelings in a group is dangerous. Remember how the son of Our Lord was much opposed in his sanctity."

Mr. Butler leaps from his pew. He points directly at me. His signs are choppy with anger.

"That girl is no child of God!"

Mrs. Pye hands baby Lissy to Mr. Pye and faces Mr. Butler while Mama, Papa, and I sit stock silent in shock.

She twirls her open hands at either side of her head. "Are you mad, sir?"

"I know what I know!" he insists.

Reverend Lee has stopped preaching and raises his hands in a sign of peace, but he no longer has his congregation's attention. Sarah looks sullen that her performance was interrupted.

"And what do you know?" Mrs. Pye inquires. "You nasty toad!"

Everyone except my family is on their feet, facing one another in strife.

"She took the children to the field," Nancy's mother signs. I've almost never seen her speak before her husband. "The Wild Goat Man Field."

Is that what they're calling it now? I burst into laughter.

"Look at her laughing!" Old Widow Tilton, who I thought was a friend, intones.

Mrs. Pye reads my mind. "How do you expect her to act? These accusations are cruel and slanderous."

The hint of legal scandal momentarily stifles Mr. Butler and the Skiffes.

Papa stands.

He is a thoughtful signer, using an economy of words.

"Many of you know my daughter since born. You

aware I lose my son. What do you mean to take from my family now?"

Some parishioners sit down, the spite taken out of them.

Mr. Skiffe faces Papa. He's always resented the respect my father commands.

"Your daughter brings havoc," he signs exaggeratedly. "Not just as a schoolteacher, but the way she stares oddly at nothing with a devilish intensity. She was corrupted by her dealings off-island."

Mrs. Pye seems ready to pounce, but she pauses as Mama stands. It is highly uncommon for her to contribute to town gatherings.

"How dare you, sir!" she signs with dignity. "My daughter was kidnapped. You blame her for events not of her making."

This settles most of the group and Reverend Lee looks to take the reins again.

Mrs. Skiffe will not let Mama have the last word. "Mary led my Nancy astray! Neither of them has a young man or is skilled at homemaking. It's unnatural."

Mama signs to me and Papa. "It's time to return home. I have a pudding on the stove."

As Papa hugs me to his side, Mama walks with head held high in front of us. Everyone moves aside. Reverend Lee approaches her before we exit.

"I apologize," he signs, rubbing a hand on the right side of his chest.

She treats him kindly. "I asked for a baptism. I didn't expect it to be one of fire. You will come visit me and give me all the details of the voyage. I believe you were acting in our best interests. My cherished daughter is being cast out. Together we will pray for her safe passage."

Several people attempt to make eye contact with me. I look down as I leave. Lifelong bridges have been burned. I couldn't bear to see one of the strange visions now. Would it prove I am the oddity they see me as?

Chapter Eleven

Mama decides to make the preparations fun. We separate my clothing into groups around my room and choose from each pile the most appropriate: a warm-weather dress, a bonnet, boots for the city and for the countryside. She holds up one faded blue homespun gown that she made for me to do winter chores in. "Dour," I sign.

"You must appear your most pious," she retorts. "No frippery for you on this voyage."

She is right. It's the opposite of when I prepared to leave for the Vale, when I borrowed Sarah Hillman's fancy trunk and packed the finest of my own belongings. To the missionaries, dressing as plainly as possible speaks to a charitable and selfless nature. I've been taught that it shows wealth has been passed on to the less fortunate. Still, I know of some who think the suffering of the poor is next to godliness, an idea that sits ill at ease with me.

"Should I hide my sense of humor too?" I

wonder aloud, fingers moving without thought. What will it be like, traveling with the missionaries? How much of my true self must I keep hidden? Will my patience last for months on end? They will expect it, so I must try.

I look up to see Mama smiling at me softly. She cups my cheek. "Who would my Mary be without that wry streak of hers?"

I return her smile with no small amount of wonder. How is it that this has brought us closer together than ever?

Mama has emptied her plain wooden sewing box for me to use as a trunk. She lined it with extra fabric, so my clothes won't snag on the unfinished wood. The missionaries will expect no less—or more—of me than to be so humble in the face of the world.

I also know that they have limited room to offer me on their ship, so what I pack in the trunk is all that can come with me. Papa has offered me a leather satchel to hold my journal, so it will not get wet in the sea's often unpredictable and perilous weather. I tuck it against the inside wall of the trunk.

Mama surveys our work. "Will this be enough?"

"I suppose it'll have to be," I reply. "Anyway, I'm bringing less than our ancestors migrated with."

"Oh, don't believe that," she says with a small smile. "How do you think my grandmother's cupboard came to be here?"

She startles a laugh out of me. I'm glad to know I am leaving with matters at peace between us.

Sitting down to tea, Reverend Lee reminds Mama, "This is not a dangerous excursion, but one of healing and education."

"I hope so," she signs, her fingers flying like birds.

"I've spoken to the friends we met in Tisbury, Mary. I'm afraid you'll have to sail with them from Boston Harbor. I know you have unpleasant associations with the place."

"It's just a place," I try to convince myself.

"You'll take her across the Cape like last time?" Mama signs.

"I will be busy, but I'll find a trusted friend," Reverend Lee signs.

"I must visit Beatrice in Mashpee," I sign.

Reverend Lee signs, "If you mean to do so, you'll have to leave quickly to give yourself time."

"Who will take me there?" I inquire.

"Let me talk to the Tisbury parish again. I'm sure a local fisherman can take you the short distance to the Cape. I'll see if anyone in the league will dare to pick you up from a Wampanoag village."

Mama asks, "Is this absolutely necessary, Mary?"

I look into her sky-blue eyes. She meets my gaze.

I lower the wall as she described it, to show her the intense concern and affection I carry for this remarkable girl who was treated so badly for not being able to hear.

I trace my finger across my neck to remind her of the ligature mark left by Beatrice's mother when she attempted to end Beatrice's life.

A tear runs down Mama's face and into her teacup. She swishes the salty drop into the sweet brew and nods, almost imperceptibly.

I tell Reverend Lee, "I don't want to march in as an uninvited colonizer."

"It may be tricky to gain permission. I'll try to find a fisherman going that way who has ties to the tribe.

So as not to draw attention to you or Beatrice, you'll likely have from sunup till sundown together."

Mama signs to me, "Don't forget you need to extend an invitation to Miss O'Neal. She will stay here, at least initially. I cannot bear to have George's—and now your—bedroom empty again."

"I think you'll find her delightful, Mama."

"If you say so."

I hesitate. "You know she's Irish . . ."

"I will personally introduce her to good townsfolk who will help in her research," Mama signs. "She has helped you out of more than one scrape, and I owe her my gratitude."

This is generous of Mama. Though I recognize it's unlikely she'd extend the same courtesy to my Wampanoag friends.

Mama sighs and gives me a skeptical look.

"Get it off your chest," I urge, releasing my tightly closed fists.

"It's a good thing you cannot speak—and the missionaries cannot sign! Before they begin to learn our language, they won't be subjected to so many of your opinions and cheek!"

"Mama, I'm shocked! I never interject my ideas until I am asked or invited! Nor do I show impertinence to my elders!"

"Fiddlesticks," she signs with a mischievous expression.

Reverend Lee nods with some amusement. Mama interprets his speech. She's the more skilled signer, and it's faster when she speaks for him. Besides, our family's unique signing seems to confound him.

"Mary, you will have to be careful around these people. You'll need to keep your own counsel. I have told them no more and no less than they need to know. Miss Mitchell seems very taken with you, but you're different in so many ways. Write your keen observations of the crossing and the education of the deaf in Europe. You may find a companion. But don't become involved in intrigue."

Mama signs, "What intrigue could she encounter on the Continent?"

"France has forcibly occupied Spain, formerly their allies. Napoleon Bonaparte has installed his own brother in place of the king. England has answered and come to Spain's defense in their long-standing quarrel with Bonaparte. Lieutenant General Arthur Wellesley of the British Army leads England's forces in a land war on the Iberian Peninsula. After decades of fighting, tensions are reaching a breaking point, and men are suspicious. I would avoid mentioning France in England, and vice versa, even with the protection of the missionaries."

Mama is a Yankee through and through. She throws her hands up before signing, "I'll be happy when you've passed through England and reach France. The less time spent with the royalists the better. But be safe. Do what Reverend Lee tells you."

It's clear she finds the situation worrisome, but she pretends not to for my sake. I often forget that Mama was born in wartime America. I've never thought of what she must have seen and felt when she was growing up. She's brave to let me go.

"I will mind that," I sign.

Mama turns her attention back to the packing. "What else is left to do?" she signs.

"There's someone who needs one more lesson before I go—and someone I must speak to."

Chapter Twelve

Before I search out Liam, I walk down the high road carrying a letter to Miss O'Neal. I'm sending a simple message. She will discover my departure when she arrives. I don't want my absence to keep her away.

Dear Nora,

What a relief it was to receive your correspondence!

I've spoken to my parents, and you are welcome in our home. If you use your straightforward charm, I think you'll find townsfolk are more likely to cooperate with you and your studies than they were with Andrew Noble.

Send us your traveling schedule when you're ready.

Vineyarders may be able to help in your passage from Cape Cod to the island. Our door and hearts are open to you!

Sincerely,
Mary Lambert

A sailor on the beach tucks it into a dry pocket of his sealskin coat. His signing is more spare than Papa's. A ripple of understanding passes between us when he makes the sign for "city." He will be in Boston soon. He'll make sure it reaches Nora.

Walking on, I see Ezra Brewer's old house—a cabin, really—in the distance. If it was ramshackle in his lifetime, it's dilapidated now. The gray roof has turned to the color of an artichoke. The sea air will do that. I haven't visited often, though my friend extended the offer on his deathbed.

The last time I wandered down and peeked in the windows, everything looked to be where he'd left it— his one fork, plate, and cup on the table, his heavy rain hat hanging on a peg. Since he rarely invited guests inside during his lifetime, it felt disrespectful to enter afterward.

Still, Ezra Brewer's home comforts me. I see no imaginary shapes in brimstone here. Just the former lair of one who lived life by his own rules and the rhythm of the tides. What did he tell me? "You were always my horse in the race." He'd want me to show the French deaf what's what.

I gallop as fast as my legs will take me back to our farm.

Eamon is standing by the sheep shelters. He's holding a rake, stretching his shoulders and yawning. I don't like when people shake me to get my attention, so I wait for him to notice me.

He does not startle. He knows why I'm here. He points to the loft in the barn.

I climb carefully, clutching my skirt in place. Oh, to be a girl again when it didn't matter if I hiked up my dress! I sense rustling above me and pray this child does not make me a fool when I'm here to help him.

Near the top, I spy the boy sitting cross-legged. I signal him not to run off. He waits for me until we are both seated on damp hay. He doesn't look up but strokes Yellow Leg's fur. Once a scrap of kitten Ezra Brewer gave me, she's now more Liam's companion than mine.

"I'm leaving," I tell him. "But I want you to keep up your studies. I'll give you a book to work through. If you have any questions, ask my papa."

He shakes his head, wrinkling his nose.

"Why not?" I sign.

He shrugs his shoulders.

"I know you are upset that you tried to share your beliefs and heritage with the class and were banished from the school."

He finally signs. "I'm used to it."

"No, no," I insist, shaking my head and fist. "Don't you ever get used to it!"

He lets his stubbornness slip and tears fill his eyes.

"Yes," I sign. "Feel strongly the injustice done to you. And do something about it. Educate yourself. You are my brightest pupil."

He watches my sign for "bright" flicker in the air. He bites his knuckles while thinking. Then he nods.

"Promise me?"

This time he looks into my eyes. I know this child cannot tell a lie. He's almost too transparent, like a grassy pond illuminated by sunlight.

"I was the teacher, and I learned something from you," I sign. "About Beltane. What was it you said?"

He looks around and shakes his head.

"It's safe," I promise, tapping my lips and my heart.

He repeats in speech: "Beannaich, a Thrianailt fhioir nach gann."

Looking at me, he thinks before interpreting it into sign. "It's the beginning of the Beltane blessing. 'Bless, O Threefold true and bountiful . . .'"

"I wish *I* had three languages," I sign.

Not able to take the compliment, he sticks out his tongue. I return the gesture. We're on equal ground again!

Uplifting Liam makes me wonder how far I'll stretch my words. Walking down the high road toward a friend's house, I'm ready to explore what it is I hope to achieve. And how far I'll go to get it.

I've wanted to see the Paris school for the deaf since Mrs. Pye first told me about it: a large school for girls and boys, where everyone signs, including great thinkers who share their philosophy. I long to see the same in America! How much I could learn to bring back and spread the word. We're a new nation, but we mustn't let the deaf languish, maltreated and isolated.

Still, Reverend Lee's advice on following my heart no matter the consequences worries me. I understand he's a cleric. A good man, who once owned slaves, then repented. His ideas about compromise may come from being a man of the world. But I'm seeking a mentor who always puts justice first, while not being afraid to get her hands dirty.

Mrs. Pye is pacing in her yard as I approach the quaint, well-kept house next to her husband's blacksmith shop. I'm hesitant to interrupt her, but there might not be another chance for us to talk alone before I depart.

I stretch my arms above my head and bend down to touch my toes. She quickly catches sight of me. She stops moving and looks at me with a big grin, before waving me inside. I sit in her front parlor as she prepares tea and brings a tray with scrumptious lemon cake.

Her signing is broad and expressive, as though she is still teaching in the classroom, yet intimate for me.

She pours the tea, then signs, "I was wondering if you'd come. I love being a wife and mother, but I sometimes feel constricted. Hence my brisk walk to assess our property. The baby's asleep."

"I often feel the need to be free. Sometimes I imagine myself running without stopping."

She nods rather than teasing me. "At your age, I used to sprint up and down the beach, shouting that I would change the world."

"You opened up the world to me."

"You're kind, Mary." She leans back in her chair, sipping milky tea and watching me. "What can I tell you now?"

"Reverend Lee says that as we grow, we are given opportunities which can advance our goals to help others, but, at the same time, may hurt those we love."

Mrs. Pye leans forward, her hands moving rhythmically as knitting needles.

"The hardest thing I've learned is that it's impossible not to hurt anyone. There are some who make a career of performing charity, but it's mostly vanity. While our old friend Ezra Brewer shook his fist at the Almighty, he left a crater in our hearts."

Taking a quiet moment to honor Ezra Brewer with a friend gives me fortitude. "These missionaries would be appalled at how my father raised me, yet I'll never regret that!"

"You were lucky that your father is one of the few in our town who hired the Wampanoag as paid laborers, including the freedman Thomas Richards, who probably taught you as much as I did!"

"I am happy to know him," I sign. "You are right that he took time out of his farm work to engage with me. He challenged me and told me things I wouldn't know otherwise."

"In the hopes that you'd grow up to be different, more just. Even a friend who speaks the truth."

Am I? I feel a little shaky and change the subject. "Why do you say I'm lucky?"

"My father was cruel to slaves and Indians, and because I adored him, I believed what he said and didn't question his terrible actions."

"I never knew that about you," I sign. "You stand up for justice!"

"Not always," she signs. For a moment she can't meet my eyes and her hands idle in her lap. "I had to learn what you were given by your father and nurtured with your own natural curiosity and compassion. Don't throw it away only to have to find it again."

"I'm going to see Beatrice, my first pupil from the Vale, before I join the missionaries."

Mrs. Pye signs, "I'm sure she'll be glad to see you."

I break out in a big smile and shake my head and fist.

"But," Mrs. Pye signs, weighing each word. "What do you hope to find there?"

"In Mashpee?"

"Yes."

"Like you said, to reunite with my young friend and see her family and village again."

"Obviously you will tell them about your voyage."

"Of course. I mean, I know the missionaries seek to convert Indians from their traditional beliefs, but Beatrice will understand I'm traveling with them to have access to the Paris school for the deaf, where I can learn to help others."

Mrs. Pye's quick signs hit me like rocks. "They don't *seek* to convert. They leave no choice and force assimilation. You believe you'll avoid hurting them, as Reverend Lee predicted?"

"They know me. It's my only way to get there!"

Mrs. Pye looks me up and down.

"And if Thomas were joining a group who purposefully harmed the deaf?"

"He'd never do that! You're confusing me!"

"Mary, you want those in Mashpee to give you

their permission, to tell you it's all right to betray them. It's understandable at your age, but be aware—"

I cut her off. "No, no, no!" She purses her lips but does not further pursue the subject as I hastily say goodbye and thank her for her advice. I am certain my friends will understand. So why am I running from her now?

I look back to wave farewell. She is standing by the gate to her yard, uncommonly still. I give her a forced smile before hurrying home.

Mama welcomes me with open arms. She pats my back when I tell her about seeing Liam. While she prepares my favorite cranberry bread, I sit at the kitchen table, slowly inhaling and exhaling. I imagine I'm blowing clouds around the sky. I can decide my own fate, can't I?

Chapter Thirteen

The day before my departure, Mrs. Pye stops by with the remainder of her lemon cake. Mama invites her in for tea. She says she can't stay but just wanted to pop around one last time to say goodbye. It's obviously a peace gesture, but I feel cool around her.

There's a question I meant to ask at her home before our conversation went awry.

"What was the name of the deaf Frenchman, the gentleman teacher your brother-in-law, Daniel Trees, mentioned?" Mrs. Pye's sister died soon after she and Daniel Trees married. Mrs. Pye can hardly speak of it. But her brother-in-law's visits bring joy whenever the wind blows his sails in our direction.

Mrs. Pye rises to leave, hugs Mama, and nods at me. "If I remember correctly, his name is Laurent Clerc. Tell him 'Bonjour' from me!"

Mama gets into the spirit. "There is a museum that George always wanted to visit in Paris . . ."

"The Louvre!" I finger-spell, letting my guard

down. "I will get there, and I'll look for Monsieur Laurent Clerc," I assure our guest as we bid her goodbye.

When my departure day finally arrives, I feel so alive with purpose I forget all about my spat with Mrs. Pye. I convince Mama and Papa not to see me off. I feel old enough to give our kisses and embraces at home and walk down to the beach alone, head held high, in case my enemies are secretly keeping watch.

This is my journey, my choice. I am setting off by myself for the first time without a familiar chaperone and beyond all boundaries I've previously crossed. Whatever mistakes I make or successes I achieve are mine to own.

A sailor I recognize but don't know loads my trunk onto his slender vessel. He nods and points. I'm not anxious to make conversation. I climb aboard without his assistance and decide to stand, until the waters get rough. I want to see where I'm going and what I'm leaving behind.

Before the Vineyard is out of sight, I turn to face it, grasping a rope to keep balance. I imagine myself a little older than I am now, as I raise my chin and keep my face set—even as the wind blows against me. I don't want to appear like a child when I see Miss Mitchell again.

The receding island looks dark in shadow. A sleeping giant turning his back to me. Then the boat pivots, and it comes alive again. Glancing up at the cliffs, I see a group of villagers standing near the edge. They lift their hands into the air, and I realize they've come to see me off. My heart pounds in my chest as I wave both arms over my head.

Home.

I rush to each side of the vessel to memorize every detail, even as it disappears on the horizon. The smaller it becomes, the more I realize that I let a handful of bad apples at the Meeting House have too much power over me. I will return to the town and friends I call my own.

But first, there are miles and miles of uncharted territory ahead.

Chapter Fourteen

Beatrice is nearby.

I ride to Mashpee in a cart driven by a former student of Reverend Lee. He's uncommonly tall with a pronounced Adam's apple that bobs, and much fancier rags than most novices I've met. He knows few signs but enough to understand my intent. When we reach Sandwich, the oldest town on Cape Cod, I ask to slow down to observe the grist mill. It was named after a town in Kent, England, where my ancestors come from.

Before contact, this land was inhabited by Algonquin-speaking Wampanoag, who suffered great losses due to virgin soil epidemics, or infectious diseases spread by Europeans, against which they had no immunity. Also devastating were King Philip's War and conversion efforts that pushed them into Praying Towns. They are still fighting for their rights.

My lanky, bobbing host seems hesitant to stop, so I stomp my feet on the floorboard. He comes to a slow halt. I nod, realizing I no longer feel intimidated by every hearing person I meet off-island. He smiles politely, but I imagine he's muttering to himself.

I debark to take in the full height of the grist mill. In 1640, Plymouth Colony granted Thomas Dexter six acres to build it on Shawme Lake. It sits beside tranquil Lower Shawme Pond. A cut-stone channel, called a millrace, steers the waters of the rushing Mill Creek into a relentlessly revolving wooden waterwheel that is moved by the natural momentum of the current. The churning paddles provide the energy that makes the grindstones within turn, grinding corn to meal.

Watching the wheel go around is soothing, and something about the water sluicing over it makes me feel cleansed, as if it is washing over me.

I can feel the power of the factory, a hum of vibration in the air that almost makes my hair stand on end, like the thrill before a lightning storm. The creek sends small tremors through the ground. It's different from standing on the beach, where the sand seems to absorb most of the impact of the incoming tides. There is no end to my love of stimulating experience!

I return to my driver, and we move on. He stops at the edge of the small town that I visited with Nancy's uncle Jeremiah when we brought Beatrice back to her father's people. The driver gestures for me to get out and walk. He doesn't even step down to help me untie my trunk and steady it in my arms. I hoist it out of the carriage and set it in the sand so I can exaggeratedly sign "thank you." I bring my open palm forward from my chin, but my face wears a grimace. I promised to be on my best behavior, but I won't suffer fools who don't like deaf girls or Indians.

A sailor was supposed to deliver a message to Beatrice and her family so they could estimate when I'd arrive. But I see no one.

The houses are huddled together in the distance. I was worried that Mrs. Pye's words would sour my mood, but I feel excited to be back here. I walk alone, lugging my small trunk. It's good practice for my journey abroad. I remember the rhyme Ezra Brewer used to spook me before I met Beatrice: "Ladybird, ladybird, Fly away home, Your house is on fire, And your children all gone."

I hold my breath in my cheeks, squeeze my eyes tight, and say a silent prayer. *Her wounds are fresher than mine. Let her be well.*

As I approach her home, I reflect on my first time here. I was an unexpected and not wholly welcome outsider. But Beatrice's affection toward me made the townspeople less suspicious of my presence. A part of me feels foolish remembering that experience. I was more certain of my mind then, but with less knowledge of my position.

I spy a wisp of chimney smoke in the air and follow the rich cooking smells until I am standing outside the dwelling of a woman I recognize as Beatrice's aunt. She extends a friendly hand and leads me inside. Perhaps I wasn't a complete ninny in the past.

My embarrassment over how I appear to these good people evaporates when I realize I'm about to see Beatrice again. I'm knocked sideways—with greater force than the rhythm of the grist mill, or even Reverend Lee's announcement of the opportunity to travel to the Continent.

This moment is my tabula rasa. George taught me the concept of the Greek philosopher Aristotle. It means a blank slate waiting to be written on and given direction. Mine is not literal, but in my head.

Beatrice is sitting on a bench in a round room and

looks up when I enter. I rush to her side and see her lips move as my hands fly with questions. We stop and laugh. She takes my hand in hers—it feels small and rough, with calluses on the edges of her fingers—and we swing our arms between us.

It is a childlike way to say hello with great affection, like a hug. It reminds me that she is still very young despite her great trauma.

Though silent communication is possible, it would be better to have someone with several languages. Is there anyone here?

Chapter Fifteen

Thomas Richards enters the room smiling. I didn't expect to see him here. He is a welcome surprise as well as a warm and inviting presence. He puts his hand on Beatrice's head in a tender way, and she grins up at him.

I sign, "The second time we've met in this town!" The last time I saw Thomas, I was bringing Beatrice home, and he was getting ready to board a whaling ship. But after Uncle Jeremiah abandoned me, Thomas chose to return to his daughter Sally and took me home instead. I like to think we're friends.

"I was called when we knew you were coming."

I clearly see affection between him and Beatrice. Have they become close? "You're spending a lot of time here?"

"Don't mind about that," he signs with a wink.

I lay out my journal, a pen, and ink on a table. Beatrice and I use pantomime. Thomas looks back and forth. The intuitive deaf communication is unfamiliar to him.

She begins our exchange. "Your hand is cold."

"You've grown—two, no, three inches." She's catching up to me quickly.

"You're the same size."

I stick my tongue out at her playfully. "Your hair has grown." She now has two long braids. She tugs on one.

"You're thinner." It's true, my appetite has decreased of late. I poke my tummy.

"Your eyes are brighter." Always keen, Beatrice's gaze now dances with a light I did not see when she was in captivity, but I detect a glimmer of darkness behind it.

"You look tired."

Do I? I suppose I must, after everything I've gone through. Even without knowing the trials I've endured lately, she sees it in me. She's always been a watcher of the world, an observer.

"You look sad," I note. Not so keenly noticed on my part. Of course she is sad, after everything *she* has been through. After being abducted to Boston, my experiences haunted me every day. And I didn't live through what she has. It'll take time, and care, which she has an abundance of here.

"You're dressed plainly," she writes. I brush a hand down my homespun dress. My face tightens. How will I broach the topic of the missionaries?

I quickly put away my writing supplies as Beatrice's aunt brings in a satisfying meal of shellfish and the savory round bread she served me on my first visit here. Thomas introduces her as Caroline and squeezes her waist in thanks. The corners of my mouth turn up. He catches my look and signs for me to "hush," but I can see he's pleased. The loss of his wife, Helen, struck him deeply.

"Sally's papa and now Beatrice's too?" I sign.

"Food." He taps his fingertips on his lips.

I realize I'm hungry. Beatrice and I eat in silence—our eyes locked like when we were student and teacher, but now on equal footing. I was worried we'd have to work to establish a friendship, but there's a strong bond from our history. Each of us is trying to investigate the other, to see past the superficial details and weigh each other's soul.

Caroline and Thomas do not break our gaze with conversation. Her auntie seems to be curiously observing a side of Beatrice she hasn't seen before. I don't recall meeting other deaf people when I attended a Mashpee town meeting last time I was here, though there must be elders who have lost hearing. While Beatrice and I have our languages, whether sign or speech, the sense of sight is powerful in us.

Caroline dispels the intensity when she stands up to clear the table.

Thomas interprets for us, moving smoothly between languages.

"The meal was delicious," I sign. "Thank you."

"I set the nets and traps for fresh fish in the morning," Beatrice says.

"Oh, I've never done that."

She looks amused by my ineptitude.

"I haven't seen Sally in a while," I sign. "Will she marry her beau?"

Thomas chuckles and rubs the stubble on his chin. "He's chasing her around, all right. But she seems content to keep independent, even as she helps the Aquinnah community and tends to animals up and down the Vineyard."

"Even my neighbors' prejudices do not stop them

from consulting her on their livestock," I note. "She is the best there is."

He nods with pride.

Beatrice is watching our sign talk without great interest. When I pause—am I chatting nervously with Thomas?—she comes to the point.

"Why did you come here?"

"I wanted to see how you're doing. I think about you constantly."

Beatrice nods slowly. I feel she thinks of me often too, and with concern.

"Thomas said you're the schoolteacher in your town. Why did you leave your students?"

"Why don't you show me your village? I'd love to walk along the shore." I sign so sloppily that Thomas has trouble interpreting.

"But—" she says

"I remember you were skilled at art," I interject, Thomas's hands moving deftly. "Does it still interest you?"

Beatrice's eyes light up. She stands and gestures for me to follow her into the room where she sleeps. It is filled with wonders!

Remarkable drawings—outlined in charcoal and filled in with brilliant pigments—line the walls. Beatrice's talent is growing and becoming more refined.

She leads me from picture to picture, while Thomas continues to interpret. I almost recognize these images that she's put onto paper; they're a whisper of the visions I've been having.

"At first, I watched the horizon every day," she says. "I thought they'd come to take me back to that prison."

"It was worse than that!" I sign, then calm my temper and cross my hands. I realize this is her story, and I need to let her tell it.

"For weeks, I thought I felt horses, stampeding, coming my way. They looked like they were made of bones. Dead things without eyes or flesh. Auntie would shake me awake and ease my dreams. But I waited every day for those people in the big house to return."

I marvel that something so terrifying can be beautifully rendered.

"Then, after months, I started to forget. I ate more

and grew stronger. I did chores with Auntie. My little cousins wanted me to play with them in the small ponds and inlets. We laughed when the frogs jumped, and small fish tickled our toes."

These images make me smile. I glance at the wall and am glad to see she's left blank space to draw her future.

"Finally, I stopped fearing the return of outsiders."

I sigh in relief, but she isn't finished.

"Then I realized it's that thing." She points to an image of the Meeting House made with overlapping circles of charcoal, lacking color.

"Its windows watch me like eyes. The black door swings open like a flapping mouth. I will never be free of it, and what happened outside its doors."

Though the room is warm, I shiver.

She touches the scarf covering the scar on her neck. The constant reminder that her mother who grew up in that elegant prison tried to be rid of her.

Thomas holds her shoulders with the same gentleness that he cradled a new pony on our farm.

"It takes time to heal," he signs and speaks.

"My body?" she says.

"And the spirit," he adds.

She vigorously shakes her head.

"I'm not telling you to forget. Images of cruelty and the sound of sorrowful cries from my days in enslavement will never leave me. They keep me awake some nights, but I honor all my experiences."

"I couldn't choose what I wanted!" I see her cry out as Thomas signs. My heart is throbbing in my throat.

"That's true," he signs and speaks. "I'm sorry, little one."

She closes her eyes and releases a quick breath.

She turns to me and says, "I thought you were the bravest person in the world. You went into that filthy room and tried to teach me. I knew finding a way to tell you was my only chance. You brought the pen and paper. I wrote my name. You could have run away and left me there. But you came back."

My conversation with Mrs. Pye leaps to the forefront of my mind. But it's no longer just ideas about what is right. My friends are standing in front of me, and they deserve the truth.

Chapter Sixteen

"Missionaries..."

I know no sign for the word, so I write it on a blank page in my journal.

I have walked out the front door with them following me. It's clear that place is Beatrice's sanctuary, and it somehow feels like I'd be sullying it with talk of the league.

They both look at me questioningly, not understanding why I'm suddenly broaching this particular topic. I wring my hands.

"I've been given an offer," I sign. I notice Thomas is more hesitant in his interpreting. "A league of American missionaries is voyaging abroad, passing through Europe to the Middle East and Asia. I've been given the chance to travel with them, protected."

Thomas's and Beatrice's alarmed reactions cause me to add hastily, "Of course I'd never even consider it if it didn't give me the opportunity to visit the deaf school in France! It's not as if I'll be joining their mission!"

I feel my shoulders slump as I try to explain. "It's all that I've wanted. For years now, since I was first told of the school. I'm hoping to observe and learn from them, so that I might bring their methods back to our fledgling country. To help those who didn't grow up in advantageous circumstances, as I did."

Beatrice shakes her head and talks to Thomas while keeping an eye on me.

"What did she say?" I ask him hesitantly.

He interprets for both of them. "Never trust colonizers forcing their beliefs."

I am rebuked by his blunt words and suddenly feel defensive. "I understand about the Praying Towns . . ."

Thomas interrupts while Beatrice's gaze remains fixed on me. "Mary, you can never fully understand the destruction by Europeans and their descendants. They made themselves rulers of this land and of those who have always lived here. Their self-appointed mission is to threaten the Wampanoag away from our old ways—and try to make us act, look, and think like them."

I shake my head. "That's not my intention! I'm visiting deaf schools in Europe. This is likely the only way I can get there. I can influence them! If I can educate the missionaries about the deaf, I can surely teach them how harmful their attitude is toward Indians!"

"They won't bring you back, Mary," Beatrice says with touching concern, which makes me feel like a clod. "When I went to the Vale, I thought I was only traveling to my mother's people for a short period of time. I never imagined I'd be taken captive."

That's information I didn't have before. Poor Beatrice! So cruelly deceived. Is this what will happen at the Indian mission school that the league is planning to build? After they close the doors, will the children inside become prisoners?

My advantages become clear, and I quickly reply. "I've thought of that," I sign. "I mentioned it to my friend who introduced me to the missionaries. He seemed to think they'd keep their word and let me return home."

"Except during your ordeal in Boston," Thomas signs plainly, "you've been sheltered by your family and town. You've done right by me and Sally, and

Helen when she was alive. Your father taught you well. Then you brought Beatrice back home at risk to your own life and reputation. Whom you select to associate with from now on is up to you. I will not condemn your choices, but I will not sanction them either. That's all the counsel you'll get from me on the subject."

I recoil, chastened. Thomas was always one of my teachers. What more could I expect?

Beatrice nods slowly. "And will these deaf schools' teachings—when you bring them back—include young ones like me?" She is clear-eyed as she looks me right in the face.

"It is my goal to educate all," I assure her. "On that I have not wavered."

Still, I feel split down the middle, and am relieved when Thomas changes the subject. He points to a sandbar in the distance and tells me Beatrice is determined to take me there.

Is it possible to travel with Miss Mitchell and also keep my friends here?

Chapter Seventeen

The sandbar is quite wide, ranging from fifty to one hundred feet in width. Even though the tide is low, I know we can become stranded if we go out at the wrong time in the tidal cycle.

A year ago, I learned that lesson the hard way, and would have become part of the seafloor if my friend Sally had not come to my rescue. It takes only a few minutes for the waters to rise. I shake off the memory and walk the shoals with Beatrice. I trust she knows this place well and doesn't fear peril.

She bends down to create drawings in the sand. I'm fascinated by the way she brushes her stick instead of pressing it firmly. One study looks like a flock of birds taking flight. Just as I'm trying to figure out its meaning or if it's part of a larger image, she smooths the sand with the palm of her hand. I startle, feeling distressed that she erased the image. But she looks up and crinkles her nose. It wasn't her finest work—something I can identify with as a writer.

And the league of missionaries will build schools to teach Indian children skills? This girl puts such notions to shame!

What can I do to entertain her, like my students in Chilmark? I think of a sign she'll understand and indicate antlers with splayed hands on my head. I stomp my feet, like a lively herd.

Beatrice grins at the memory. She imitates our struggle in the deer park at the Vale. We prance together, seeing who can appear more fawn-like. It's the lightest I've felt since Nancy and I pretended to be spies in our youth, lurking behind our hometown's high wall and climbing trees to look for clues.

When we stop laughing, Beatrice points to me. Her eyes are sharply focused with her eyebrows raised questioningly. Now that we are alone, I feel she wants to know how I've been affected by all that's happened to me. She is the easiest person to tell, except we don't share a language! But she's perceptive. She has been reading me since I arrived.

I exaggerate my hand signs and use my eyes and body to full effect.

I see things
Not dreaming
Awake
Bits of fire
house, church, horse's eye
Burning
Inside me
Fear
Cannot stop
Must leave again
Look for thing
Help me
HEAL

Beatrice repeats the sign for "heal," bringing her hands off her body into fists, as if she's pulling out all the sorrow. She points to both of us.

The surf tickles my ankles. I notice the tide coming in. The shoals are flooding! I turn to race for the shore, but Beatrice grabs my wrist. Her grasp is strong. I try to pull away and point toward the beach in the distance. She shakes her head and says a word I can't recognize.

I pull harder, but she tugs back. The sun is implacable in the sky. Where is Thomas? I panic. My knees are underwater! I can't believe she means to drown me rather than let me go with the missionaries. Perhaps it's only a child's game. *What's her plan?*

At once, Beatrice lets go of my wrist, then she runs. She has a faster stride. I stand motionless, wondering if she will block my way.

Of course not! She waves to me urgently. I run, but the tide swirls around me. It means to pull me down. Beatrice is ahead of me, on sand that hasn't flooded yet. I push to reach her.

Suddenly, we are running together ahead of the waves. She looks at me and smiles. She is teaching me again. How to wait for the right moment. How to outrun danger. I put my whole body into the effort. Now we are racing. She slows down a moment to let me catch up, then sprints ahead. I push past the terrors that have held me hostage and dare to jump as I run. I feel free. The water trickling at the back of my feet will not overcome me.

Beatrice is ahead as we approach safe land. I pause to catch my breath when we are close to her auntie's house. I notice little ones chasing one another between the houses, an older man patching a hole in his roof, and clouds like swans drifting by with small, puffy cygnets behind them.

Beatrice quickly comes to a halt. She looks at me, but her defiance is gone. I catch the worry in her eyes. She points and I see the cause of her concern. Miss Mitchell—in her heavy cape with corn-silk hair wound around her head in a braid—looks so out of place in this landscape. Why the woolen cape on a summer beach? I would be compelled to laugh if Beatrice weren't afraid.

My friend slowly walks backward. I look from her to my traveling companion. My haunting visions have not appeared here, but now I see crimson outlining the figure in the distance like the charcoal in Beatrice's drawings. Miss Mitchell, who will not come into the village, seems to be vibrating.

Can she harm this loving home? Beatrice is still a fugitive, a runaway from indentured servitude at her white mother's manor. She might also be seen as a good candidate for a mission school. And Thomas. There are slave traders who desire to capture him.

The slate of my mind is no longer blank. Words are being written at a rapid pace, plans quickly made. I love my friends, but I can't turn down the opportunity to follow my dream to Europe and the deaf schools, even with a league of missionaries as my host.

I look at Beatrice enveloped in her auntie's arms. Thomas has come to stand with them. *They are indefensible against this one person. She is untouchable.* I'm filled with disgust and rage. But I'm also one of her. I pray they trust I will give her no details of them. Though why should they believe anything about me now?

"Will you bring my things?" I sign to Thomas. He has made his position known, and I will not try to elicit any sympathy. I quickly put on the stockings and boots I'm holding and smooth my hair. My plain clothes are hemmed round with salt water and sand. It will have to do.

Thomas stiffly hands me my trunk. I read Beatrice's expression. I'm not the bravest person anymore. I'm a traitor for my own goals. But I sense our bond isn't completely severed. I will cling to that, as I make my way in the inhospitable world.

I turn and walk slowly toward Miss Mitchell, the apparition disappearing and the woman coming into focus. She holds a certain fascination. It keeps me from lighting into her. I will not hang my head in shame for the company I keep. I meet her sapphire eyes, briefly.

When I look back, Beatrice breaks from her auntie's embrace and waves her arms overhead. I can see she is yelling from a distance. I can just make out Thomas interpreting. "Remember the shoals!" When she caught me, I remembered what it was like to be trapped—and that I shouldn't hesitate to run in dangerous situations.

I will come back here one day. I'll somehow make it right.

Part Two

England

Chapter Eighteen

In spite of my unease, my stride is sure and firm as I walk beside Miss Mitchell. She remains silent. She neither gestures to me nor shows me her countenance, though I imagine it is as grave and disapproving as the rigid line of her shoulders.

A dinghy is waiting for us at the pier, and I can see my plain wooden trunk is already aboard. The ship that will carry us over the Atlantic is too large to dock in the busy harbor, so we must make the short journey in a rowboat out to deeper waters where the vessel is anchored. I step into the skiff. Miss Mitchell follows, taking my hand to steady me, and we sit side by side on the bench as a sailor rows us out into the choppy ocean.

The craft we will voyage on is much larger and sturdier than the fishing boats I'm used to seeing fill the sea's horizons. I have to crane my neck as we approach a wall of dark wood stretching toward the sky. I think of the word "galleon," an old-fashioned term associated with pirates prowling the coast. I steal a glance at Miss Mitchell and can tell from her sober expression she would most likely scorn the thought.

I take hold of the rope ladder that hangs down from the deck and, hand over hand, begin to climb, trying not to look down as it shakes and twists in my grasp. Out of the corner of my eye, I spy my trunk tied with a rope being hauled by someone above.

Hands reach down to help me up over the railing, where I am placed onto the relative steadiness of the deck. I smooth my skirts and breathe a little easier. Miss Mitchell arrives behind me, and three others appear to greet her. I recognize them from Tisbury. The first is the older woman who looks as if she sucks lemons. The other two are young women, nearer to Miss Mitchell's age. I can tell from their glances that they recognize me as well. They steal secretive little looks at me, and I almost laugh when I realize they think they are being covert. Nancy would scoff at their attempts to spy. Gossips are never as stealthy as they believe themselves to be.

The man handling my trunk speaks at me in an exaggerated fashion and I suspect loudly. I nod as if I understand. Miss Mitchell holds up her hand and speaks for me without even looking at me. My face grows hot, but I made the bargain when I accepted this offer.

Miss Mitchell never properly introduces me to the others. Does she not realize this? Or is she positioning herself as my communicator and guarding that position? I watch as they talk but cannot understand anything in their exchange. I pull out my journal and write to Miss Mitchell that they are a small group. From their numbers in Tisbury, I thought there'd be more. She writes *Paris*, indicating they'll meet up with others there.

It would have been easier to get lost in a larger group. I could have sneaked away to write in my journal or daydream. With only five of us, there'll be more attention now.

Introduce? I write, and she gives me a small wave that says, "later." My lips purse.

Papa told me the voyage would take at least two months, more if we run into inclement weather, which is likely on the open ocean. He also told me that the currents made it easier and quicker to sail from England to America than the path I take now. I have thought about that a lot, how the same journey can be more or less difficult depending on where you start. How shall I fare on this one?

The crew appear to keep mostly to themselves. The captain and first mate approach with information, but it is not conveyed to me. The other passengers consist of two well-dressed men, one of whom I divine is a writer. As he stands on the deck, he ignores everything—including the rushing crewmen who bump him—to scribble messily in a disorderly journal.

Though it's a large cargo vessel, not a proper passenger ship, we are provided with passable accommodations complete with berths—cupboards that line the walls—and a table on the far side of the room. I'm relieved I will not have to sleep in a hammock hanging from the rafters. There are only four berths, but thankfully, it's clear from where each woman positions her trunk that Miss Mitchell and Miss Lemons intend to share one, as do the two young women. I'll have my own bunk to tuck myself into at night!

The men, curiously, are nowhere to be found.

After all the fuss of settling in is done, we return to

the common area, where a crewman delivers a tray loaded with wooden bowls, a tureen of soup, a pitcher of water, and some hard bread. The holy relics (as I secretly name my companions) pray over it while the two young men arrive to dine with us.

The writer's right index finger appears to be permanently stained with ink. I rub my own callus, which sits in roughly the same spot. I spy him numerous times scratching his nose with the end of his quill pen. I feel almost desperate to talk to him alone, to ask him so many different things! Has he been published? Does he dream of what he writes?

We are not introduced, but when he inquires after me, they must explain my situation because he begins enthusiastically writing to me, asking where I'm from and what brings me here.

The holy relics look uncomfortable and Miss Mitchell almost jealously protective. They clearly do not approve of the writer and his friend, who are young, unattached men of the arts. Surely their morals must be loose! What is their relationship? I can see I will be censored in what I say on this voyage. Is this a sign of what's to come?

Miss Mitchell writes to me later. He writes ghost stories. *When she sniffs, the disdain is plain to see on her face.* It is ungodly.

I think of George. Was he, too, ungodly because he enjoyed a scary tale? What about my haunting episode in the marsh with my best friend, Nancy, when we danced and pretended to be spirits in winding shrouds? What would Miss Mitchell think of that? Would we be judged in her eyes? Ezra Brewer, who liked to raise a fright, would be beyond the pale.

Matron and I have asked them, she writes of the writer and his companion, *to bed down with the crew so we may keep our interactions as formal and public as possible.*

Well, that explains that! I feel for a moment as if *I'm* sucking lemons, but quickly try to clear the sour expression from my face. We have put the men at a disadvantage for propriety's sake.

When the crewman comes again to clear away our dinner dishes, it's made obvious that it's bedtime. The writer's companion throws me a friendly wink before they depart. I shall call him Winks, and I interpret his gesture as assurance they'll make do with the arrangements.

I strip to my shift and clean up with some cold water in the shared washbasin. I slip between the stiff sheets of my berth, leaving the double doors open enough not to feel confined, but still with privacy.

I'm far too tightly wound to sleep after the events of the day, and my nerves vibrate like harp strings. I lie awake for a long while, thinking.

I consider the two young women, who appear to be almost identical sisters. They are the same height and near the same age, though one has chestnut-red hair and a darker, sunburned complexion while the other has locks of lighter brown, closer to blonde, and freckles over her pale nose. Their temperaments are different, however. Though neither has written to me, Chestnuts smiles more and is warmer. I even watched her engage with the writer without being prompted during our meal.

Freckles is more taciturn. I've already taken her for a tittle-tattler and that seems confirmed from the secretive way she speaks. At dinner, she held her hand over her mouth when she spoke, to hide her words. She seems to have influence over her sister, who remained silent after one of Freckles's discreet talks. Chestnuts walks a step behind her always.

The Matron must be the authoritative older lady who even Miss Mitchell defers to. I have something to call her at least!

Even though I've spent the most time with Miss Mitchell, I still don't believe I understand her fully. At the church in Tisbury where we met, she seemed excited to see me perform in sign. She had knowledge I didn't know about deaf European history. Is she not engaging me now because the journey ahead is arduous, and we have little time alone? Or was her initial interest and charm just bait to reel me in?

I drift off to sleep, my hands restlessly murmuring these thoughts.

Chapter Nineteen

I wake early to find that, though the sun is barely up, I have overslept compared to the holy relics. Still groggy, I wash and dress. Miss Mitchell barely suppresses a smile as I sluggishly draw on my stockings. I scowl, but playfully.

In our cabin, the Matron leads us in morning prayer, which is somber. At first, I sign as I pray, like always. But when the staring becomes too much, I remind myself of Papa's and Reverend Lee's warnings and keep still.

We are beckoned to the common area as the crewman finally appears with food to break our fast, porridge with fried eggs. The Matron looks a little green and puts the back of her hand to her forehead when she smells the food. Miss Mitchell supports her and urges her to drink water.

Winks arrives in time to eat. He looks worn out, with dark bags under his eyes. He's alone. *Bad night*, he writes on a piece of paper before Miss Mitchell snatches it away from me. He tries to give me a smile, but he's distracted.

After our meal, the relics have a Bible study session. They take their chairs from around the table and set them in a semicircle. Bibles in laps, they speak without regard for me. Freckles glances at me and puts her delicate hand over her mouth again as she leans sideways toward her sister. I narrow my eyes. Does she believe all deaf people read lips, or is she just showing off? My patience will only stretch so thin.

Miss Mitchell seems to sense this, and she bends toward me, the Good Book open and outstretched, showing me what she considers to be a pertinent passage. She does this several times.

I know my Bible, which is filled with charity and compassion, but I can see the relics tend only toward its lessons of penitence. A spark in Miss Mitchell seems to belie this.

By noonday, I am almost crawling out of my skin. I long to walk the deck but am told it is not safe to be alone among the rough and rowdy men of the crew. I wonder what they'd think of me sharing a mug of grog with Ezra Brewer or sitting outside his shack on the beach, feet propped up in front of a fire pit. I'm more comfortable with sailors than I am their kind.

Only when the sisters wish to breathe fresh sea air am I allowed to accompany them, but it means enduring Freckles's backhanded gossip. She fingers a chain around her neck and pulls out a locket that Chestnuts admires and touches with soft reverence. I can't see what's inside.

Despite the relics' fears, the crew doesn't pay us any heed, unless we get in their way. Then their manner is brusque with annoyance. Compared to what I've been warned of, there is shockingly little leering.

Evening is for needlepoint. I've brought no supplies, so Miss Mitchell lends me some of hers. To say my handwork is a disaster is an understatement. My small square of cloth is colored more from my pricked fingers than it is with my thread.

At supper, the writer is in good spirits. Winks still seems tired but more enthusiastic in engaging conversation. By my estimation, the relics behave quite rudely to them, considering the men are only trying to make good-natured chatter. I suspect they are as worn down by the tedium as I am. Fate did not give them friendly companions for this journey.

I am surprised when the writer passes me a note, sliding it across the tabletop. I lift my eyebrows and reach for it before Miss Mitchell can lay her own fingers down. *Keep up the good cheer, Quite Contrary*, it says. I told him my name last night. It must have conjured the nursery rhyme "Mary, Mary, Quite Contrary." *We have clear skies and calm waters. We'll reach our destination in no time.*

I feel Miss Mitchell looming heavily over my shoulder, reading as well.

We were worried when you did not breakfast with us this morning, I reply. *We* were not—I was. And from the playfully skeptical face he makes, I know he sees right through that little fib.

I like to sleep in.

Miss Mitchell is perfectly scandalized by his response and chides him vocally. I offer a shrug in apology, but his manner is mischievous, and I believe he's provoked her intentionally.

Before bedtime, we are led in prayer again. My mind drifts. I hope Nora has arrived on the island and is keeping Mama and Papa busy and in good cheer. Above all, I wish for patience. How many times have I been told to mind this necessary but dull virtue? Sometimes I feel I'll burst out in wildness, like a tiger roaming the decks!

Chapter Twenty

Each day and week are the same as the last: I see the others only at breakfast and supper. The rest of my time is filled with prayer and quiet busywork. The tip of every finger has been bled thoroughly from my notoriously terrible attempts at needlepoint.

I am lucky when any one of the relics wishes to go on deck, though the Matron is a particularly unpleasant companion.

Today, Miss Mitchell surprises me by coming to stand beside me, resting her elbows on the railing as she looks out over the sea with me while I stand and muse in peace. What will I say when I meet Laurent Clerc in Paris? Because our languages are visually based, will we have an easier time crossing sign language barriers than two people who speak different tongues?

Miss Mitchell startles me by touching my hand. I'm surprised to find that the gesture suddenly fills me with a deep longing for Mama. I suppose that will never change, even as I grow.

When we go below, Miss Mitchell hands me an article about Thomas Braidwood, a Scottish educator and the founder of Britain's first school for the deaf.

Why did she not share this sooner? I become immediately engrossed in Braidwood's pupils, including his first in 1760, Charles Shirreff. He became known as a painter of portrait miniatures. I would like to see his precise art! I learn that a family with congenital deafness from my country received their education at the Braidwood Academy in Edinburgh. An American family sent their deaf children overseas unbeknownst to our Vineyard community? Imagine that!

I read that Thomas Braidwood developed a combined system for educating deaf students, which included a form of sign language. Was it like mine? I'm sad to discover that he has been deceased for several years, which means I won't have the chance to meet him.

Dr. Joseph Watson, a nephew of Braidwood, became the first head teacher of the Asylum for the Deaf and Dumb, now located in London. He must be the administrator to whom the missionary group wrote in advance, asking for permission to visit.

I am encouraged by his quote in the article: "Persons born deaf are, in fact, neither depressed below, nor raised above, the general scale of human nature, as regards to their dispositions and powers, either of body or mind."

It remains to be seen if the holy relics are truly interested in education methods for the deaf, but I'm strongly focused on a purpose.

Chapter Twenty-One

During our second month at sea, dark clouds gather in the distance. The ship pitches from the choppy waters. I'm not sure I can endure one day longer than planned.

We will likely sail around it, the writer shares with me one night.

It is unseemly for a man to write private messages to an unmarried girl such as you, Miss Mitchell tells me later. *People will make assumptions about your character.*

She means that Freckles would tell everyone.

The burden of doubt would be on me even though he writes the letters? I'm a young woman now; I suppose I must think of these things. There is no way to tell her that I'm not interested in a suitor. It's unthinkable to any of them that I may have no regard for the romance of men.

I realize there may be an unspoken part of what she says: She views me as infirm and believes me less capable of making my own choices than a hearing woman would be. That explains her possessive attitude. Is her belief any different from Andrew Noble's, that I am little more than a live specimen to be studied?

Lightning flashes against the dark night sky and lights our berths in intervals. I feel thunder rock the ship even above the relentless rocking of the waves. I do not feel rain. Dry storms are rare. Is this some kind of omen?

The thunder persists into daylight, though with much lowered intensity. I don't think any of us got much sleep. The Matron's countenance is grave, and Chestnuts is a bit more wilted than normal, her robust complexion pale. She leans on Freckles more than usual for comfort. Even Miss Mitchell looks a little gray.

The writer is particularly wan at breakfast, with bruised hollows around his eyes. When he rests his chin in his hand, a tired Winks nudges him. I think of our first morning when Winks showed up alone. The writer had a pithy excuse then, but now it looks to be part of a more serious problem. The Matron appears to politely inquire.

The writer takes a deep breath and begins to talk.

Something urgent in me swells, and I grab Miss Mitchell's arm, giving it a tug as I silently implore her to write for me what he says. He sees this and shakes his head as he remembers me.

He is usually so impassioned, but today he slumps. I do not believe it is simply from lack of rest and am proven right. He removes a page from his journal and writes as he speaks.

I am given to having night terrors, he explains. *The first night aboard, I'm afraid I was quite disruptive and kept everyone awake. But last night was different.*

I awoke with an uneasiness. I found myself unable to move, as if something or someone were pinning my legs. For a moment, my dreams blurred the world around me, and then, in a flash of lightning, I perceived a man sitting on my legs, weighing them down. He wore a soldier's uniform, but I could not see his face. Before my eyes, he faded from view, as lightning burned away shapes in a flash of brightness.

My brother is in the military. He is the reason I am visiting England. I can only guess at the meaning of a faceless soldier, and I pray it does not bode ill. I worry for him so.

No other apparitions appeared, but I dressed and paced the deck for the rest of the night, trying to clear my head.

I see clasped hands and realize that, instead of giving sympathy, the others are praying. Unlike Reverend Lee, they do not think themselves lucky to be near a vision of the afterlife.

Before I can tuck the paper into my leather satchel, it is snatched from my hand. My head snaps around to see Miss Mitchell crumpling it. This time, I object.

I stand and stomp my foot, my hand extended, fingers wiggling impatiently as I wait to have the paper returned. Miss Mitchell is shocked. Instead of the note, I see the outline of fire in her hand. I must be making noises, because Freckles suddenly giggles behind her hand, which makes my cheeks redden. Furious, I stamp my foot again.

Despite objections, I take leave and promenade the deck on my own until I calm down. The crew spy me and smile at my fiery temperament. I catch myself signing some of the worst words I know. Ezra Brewer would be proud.

I cannot stand the thought of one more Bible study

or needlework session, and resort to desperate measures: That afternoon, I put a hand to my forehead, flutter my eyelids, and feign a faint.

Playing sick was not a trick I used often as a little girl because Mama could see right through me. Miss Mitchell and the relics are not nearly as clever. They help me into my berth and make certain I am settled and comfortable. I stretch out my "illness" to almost a week, until I can't stand being idle any longer.

I rise, dress, and join my companions, who are busy with their needlepoint. My own is snagged, and the lines are uneven. When I realize I have been recreating a pattern I saw in Beatrice's drawings, a shiver runs through me.

Have I taken the right path?

Our voyage lasts eighty-eight days. I've counted each one in my journal. In the early morning hours of the eighty-ninth day, I am woken and told we're approaching port.

The sky is lightening to a rosy pink when I spy England for the first time. The Port of Liverpool is crowded with masts like a forest of slender trees, or bony fingers reaching up for the dawn. Our ship must precariously navigate them to find our dock. Crewmen bark orders back and forth as anchor is dropped and sails are furled.

We are rowed to port in a dinghy, and I huddle with the relics. We pass between behemoths, the hulking, swaying bodies of ships that have come from all over the world.

When we reach the dock and I clamber up, the earth seems to shift beneath my feet. After months at sea, sturdy land makes me queasy.

I bid Winks and my writer friend goodbye. He hands me one final note. I thank him by bringing my hand down from my chin. He mimics the action, as does Winks, while I tuck the letter into the binding of my journal for safekeeping. I'll read it in private.

I look back at the vast ocean and then with hope to the bustling port. I've already come so far. I want to believe nothing can go wrong.

Chapter Twenty-Two

Arrival in England has a glowing effect on Miss Mitchell. Her wan pallor quickly disappears, and she seems filled with a new energy and purpose. She offers me a hand as we board a coach. Her enthusiasm sets me spinning.

Just as when I was a child on a trip across the Vineyard with Papa, I immediately press for details. It seems Miss Mitchell is now willing to converse with me at length in writing.

Can we visit the Weald first? That's where my people are from.

The area in South East England between the chalk cliffs of the North and South Downs crosses the counties of Hampshire, Surrey, Sussex, and Kent. The word "Weald" signifies woodland. I'm curious to know how close its deaf inhabitants' sign language is to Vineyard sign. It's been many generations since we crossed to the New World, and our spoken and signed languages have changed. Do any of my ancestors' families remain there? Could we still easily chat?

Miss Mitchell shakes her head.

They are members of the Church of England. There's no need for us to minister to them.

I press on the matter, but she waves it away, and I know she won't budge.

Mary, we are expected at a school for the blind in Liverpool. The children there live in darkness.

I nod and smile through clenched teeth. Contrary to widespread belief, the deaf do not live in complete silence. The vibrations of the world hum around us. I can feel this city's energy in my fingertips. I have my doubts that blind children are lost in complete darkness and am eager to discover the truth.

The school for blind children is grim. It's more like a factory with students sitting in rows and performing menial tasks. The youngest seem to be four or five years old. Where are their parents? Why would they leave their offspring in such a dismal place?

The Matron and the rest gather around the instructor (if he can be called that) and eagerly ask questions.

The children are ignored. I walk idly around them, frustrated that I can think of no way to communicate.

One girl catches my eye. She has dirty blonde hair in knotted curls. When I stop to look at the yarn she's winding, she must sense my presence because she reaches out to touch my coat. I gently pat her hand. She seizes mine. When I do not snatch it back, she turns it over to feel the length of my fingers and trace the lines on my palm. She places her hand in mine. I observe how dirty and calloused it is and am overcome with pity—no, sympathy—for this child. I wish to grab her and escape. But where to?

I feel footsteps through the crooked floorboards, and she must hear them because we quickly let go. She turns back to her work. The spark of personality I felt is hidden once again.

The principal pats my head. I wish to stomp on his foot! A flood of warning signs rises to the surface, but I force myself to hold my feelings inside. This teacher would never understand.

As I turn reluctantly to follow my group, the girl who took my hand pulls my skirt. I look back and see her point to a window. It's filthy but light filters in.

What is her message? Before I can find out, I am abruptly yanked away.

The Matron, Miss Mitchell, and the sisters shake their heads and chatter while we wait to board our carriage. My nostrils burn from fetid air.

Riding along, Miss Mitchell takes my journal and writes. *We were only meant to make a short observation there. We are expected at the Asylum for the Deaf and Dumb in London. Catch up on your rest. You have now observed how unique you are for having overcome your infirmity. Others who were not blessed have empty minds and souls.*

A crimson tint creeps like vines around all I spy. I am desperate to blot it out. I remember the pointed finger and the patch of sunlight trying to shine through murky glass. The image bursts the tint until I'm as clear-sighted as a cormorant on a cloudless day. I'm keeping up hope for Dr. Watson and his pupils. Let me look upon my deaf brethren with pride.

Chapter Twenty-Three

I start to feel fidgety as we head for Old Kent Road. Sensing my excitement, Miss Mitchell gestures for my journal and pen.

This is what we've been waiting for. Remember, they are guarded with their method, she warns me. *Though it is known that John Bolling, the American student mentioned in the article, learned to write as well as you. And he also learned speech! "I am very well and very happy," he wrote to his mother in Virginia.*

Like me, he was born deaf?

Yes, I believe so.

It can't be. I am both fascinated by and wary of this miraculous man who apparently achieved what I find impossible. For the first time, I realize that the deaf in Europe may challenge who I am rather than simply teach me.

The article also told me that the first head teacher, Dr. Watson, is Thomas Braidwood's nephew. *A desire to educate must run in the family*, I note.

She nods and writes, *And compassion for the less fortunate.* This asylum was not competing with Braidwood Academy, but rather was founded by the church for those poor souls for whom the admissions fee was too steep. It was a charitable organization for religious instruction and basic learning. In bringing Dr. Watson on, they have expanded the scope of their teaching to include Braidwood's method.

I wonder how closely his teachings reflect my kin's language in Kent. I wonder how many may have attended Braidwood's school and how it might have influenced their signs.

The asylum is a noble cause, of course. And I understand the relics' interest since it started as religious guidance by a man of God. Because of this, I will myself to ignore the fact that it is called an asylum. Perhaps it is meant in the way the church would offer it, as a sanctuary.

Even royalty donated to make the asylum a reality, Miss Mitchell writes. Solemnly, she adds, *I have been told this is where King Henry VIII persecuted those who dared to speak against him and against the religious supremacy of his rule. Martyrs were made here.* Her eyes shine. *Even if they were Catholics.*

When we arrive, we are coolly received, in spite of the letter of introduction that was sent ahead. The Matron is ushered away to speak.

While we wait, Miss Mitchell leads Chestnuts and Freckles in prayer. I join them, with one eye open, interested to see how this will unfold.

The Matron approaches us and her generally sour face seems pleased. For a moment, I see a glimmer of a sly old fox who must be a master negotiator when she is set to the task. She talks to the group, and Miss Mitchell writes for me.

They were reluctant. I told you, they are quite guarded and suspicious of outsiders. But Matron has convinced them of our pure intentions. We are not here for espionage, she teases with a small smile. But just as quickly, she is solemn again. *Mary, you will have to leave your journal outside and promise not to write of this experience.*

She must read my puzzled expression and continues. *Their conditions are not completely in the spirit of charity and goodwill, but perhaps we can win them over. I believe you may be instrumental in this. I noticed the pupils use signs that resemble your own.*

She is good at winning me over. I agree (crossing my fingers behind my back) to all of their conditions.

The school is much less lively than I'd imagined. The hallways are long and narrow, and while clean, an absence of natural light makes them appear cold and uninviting. The classrooms are better, but the children sit in solemn rows at desks. I can't imagine my students being so serious and studious!

A young, gawky teaching assistant briefly shows us around. I wonder what his qualifications are, as he has too nervous a disposition to handle unruly children.

I suspect he is either in divinity school or the only one who would take the job. Miss Mitchell writes on a slate that he is expected to be in the school from seven o'clock in the morning till eight in the evening and also with the pupils in their hours of recreation. I can't imagine!

The students we observe in the classroom are doing penmanship. It's obvious they are at different levels of proficiency. I wonder how many even have an inkling of literacy when they arrive. They keep their heads down as they copy from the Bible onto slates with deliberate concentration.

Before we are ushered out, Miss Mitchell rather daringly moves her hands to encourage me to sign. I do so, slowly at first, spelling my name and stating I'm visiting from America.

One student looks at me, startled. Then he hangs his head again to his slate. He is trying to keep focused on his studies, but his leg is twitching. There's mischief in me as I continue to interrupt their lesson. I begin explaining the Vineyard, my home, and the community we have built.

At last, he jumps out of his chair and runs to me. With excitement and apprehension, he signs quicker than I. I can't quite follow, but I urge him on and watch as he repeats my sign language in signs that are both familiar and strange to me. I feel a tingling in my toes climb up my legs and into my chest and fingers.

As a child, I asked Ezra Brewer if our Vineyard sign is the same as what was brought over from England. He replied that it had naturally changed over time, just as the hearing in America no longer speak the King's English.

This boy and I—I'll call him my cousin—are a living example of how lineage carries on and adapts.

The other students have stopped writing and look on with fascination. I learn the boy's name is Bill *Tilton* and he's from Kent! My heart bursts, overfull. If I cannot visit my family's homeland on this journey, at least I've had a little bit of it here. And won't my fellow Vineyarders—especially the family Tilton, who I grew up with!—be excited to hear this tale when I return? I will no longer be an outcast among them.

Before we can go any further, a senior teacher enters the room. He strides directly toward me, his face grave and angry. I can't blame him. I've disrupted a lesson in his classroom.

Bill once again becomes a studious pupil, and returns to his seat. He and the others continue their studies, heads down so far, their noses nearly touch their slates. I catch a few peeking under their lashes.

I am ushered out of the room with the relics, while the Matron stays behind to smooth things over. I'm less remorseful about my interruption than I ought to be.

We wait on benches in a courtyard, where Chestnuts, who usually shows no interest in my activities, questions Miss Mitchell. I can tell by her raised eyebrows.

When she turns to me, I hand her my journal, which I have kept concealed under my coat. Their disapproving looks are not lost on me, but I can see they're also curious.

Miss Mitchell writes, *What did that pupil tell you?*

His name is Bill Tilton. He's from Kent. Our signing was similar but has changed somewhat with distance and time. It took a moment to adjust to each other's dialects, and then we were interrupted.

Was it extremely hard to discern his signs?

When he signed quickly, it seemed as foreign as Greek to me. But then we slowed down to more carefully observe each other. We both use the two-handed manual alphabet, which originated here in England. Dr. Watson has made a diagram of it, which closely resembles a faded poster that used to hang in my old classroom.

Miss Mitchell writes, *I couldn't learn Greek that quickly from a native speaker. How interesting!*

I feel elated, both by the interaction with Bill and Miss Mitchell's interest.

That is, until the Matron returns stone-faced and addresses the group. From her facial expressions and body language, I discern that we are not altogether welcome in the school.

Have I made a terrible mistake by engaging the students? Wasn't that why I was brought here? And I've already made a valuable connection. I must be allowed to return!

Chapter Twenty-Four

We are given food and lodging in a room at a nearby church. Despite the sanctuary's size and opulence, we sleep side by side on cots. The windows are at street level. Feet pass at all times of day and night. Out of boredom, I try to imagine people's lives from their footwear.

Negotiations are occurring between the Matron and the deaf school. I am privy to the handwritten messages we receive.

> *Upon your first visit, we realized difficulties arise from interrupting the assistants and the pupils. It would be more appropriate for your group to commit to becoming assistants for a period of up to three years rather than our school accommodating you as guests . . .*

Three years?! The passage from Boston to England nearly grayed my hair and stooped my back. I know the holy relics don't have that time to spare.

But they are not willing to give up, and I presume they must stick to the itinerary given to them by the league and try to find a compromise. My temperament doesn't make me a natural negotiator, and the next course of action is being plotted with wagging tongues.

Of more interest to me is the boy of maybe eleven who takes our messages to and from the asylum. He rushes about looking like a little gentleman, almost. His breeches, blue topcoat, and battered tricorn look brushed but never washed. The way he tips his hat respectful-like is most amusing. The relics treat him like vermin, but I pester Miss Mitchell to tell me his name.

Irrelevant, she writes in my journal.

I turn her piety on her. *But isn't he one of God's lambs too?*

She reluctantly tells me his name is Jack. While she's inquiring, I notice him gesturing toward me. But I have to wait an entire day—we are now on our fourth—for Miss Mitchell to relay the conversation.

I told him you were deaf, she writes, *but you are a proper lady and literate, unlike him. He asked if you understood simple gestures and facial expressions. I told him not to bother you.*

Nevertheless, I make contact with Jack as he enters and leaves. He's most skilled at revealing facial expressions. I discreetly point at the letter he's carrying from the school.

His face lights up. His large blue eyes shine, his rosy cheeks flush, and his full lips open and close as if spilling over with good news. My spirits rise—perhaps we are finally getting somewhere!

Just as quickly, Jack lets his face drop. He is so crestfallen after his expressive gaiety that I decide he is a master of unspoken communication. And he finds it fun to tease me. It makes me realize how exhausting it's become to travel with no one close to my age.

I think wistfully of the clever and sometimes naughty antics of my Vineyard students and playing games with my friends. As long as we don't rebuff Dr. Watson—which I've been ready to do for some time, if they'd only give *me* the pen and ink—Jack and I can tease each other harmlessly without others taking notice. It keeps me from becoming depressed.

I watch the windows when he leaves. He has a quick gait but stops to spin in a circle or perform a quick street dance before moving on. His free spirit makes me long for a spark of adventure.

Chapter Twenty-Five

The next day, something arrives from the school that causes a stir. My interest is piqued. Can it be that we're finally moving ahead?

Miss Mitchell breaks away from an excitable Matron and leads me from the group, with all eyes on us. She glances around almost nervously, then writes, *The Matron is considering allowing you to return alone as a way for us to gain entrance. I think they mean to . . . give you oral instruction.*

Why?

They are baffled that you've never attempted speech and want to see if they can aid you. A deaf, signing instructor will be present for the experiment.

I knew I'd be a decoy. But it was my understanding I'd always be part of a group. I am extremely interested in the students, but oralization fills me with dread. *No*, I write, not knowing if I have a choice in their grand scheme.

Miss Mitchell is surprised, then demurs. *Mary*, she writes back, and I can feel the reasoned condescension in her tone. *You are so intelligent. Why hide it from the world by choosing not to communicate?*

My shoulders shoot back. My hands ball into fists. I am so overcome, I sign with my hands: "They would know what I was saying if they would listen."

She stares at me with dull, pitying eyes. I write what I have just said, and she shakes her head slightly.

I thought my signs were remarkable to you, I add.

They are, she insists. *But I don't understand why you would hamper yourself in this way. I know you want everyone to hear your voice.*

"This," I sign, "is my voice."

My face is hot. Fire blurs the edges of my vision. I can see the incomprehension in her face. Whatever argument she thought I'd put up, it wasn't this.

I speak, I write. *Who chooses to listen is a testament to their character, not mine.*

She visibly sighs. *You could make friends among the other unfortunates . . .*

I must make a sound unbidden. I am vaguely aware of how it felt in my throat. Wide eyes turn to me. The Matron holds her handkerchief over her mouth. To hide her horror, I think. In my frustration, I force out another noise. Now they have heard my voice.

Miss Mitchell folds her hands in her lap and, without saying one more word, stands and walks away from me. She may have thought I'd hesitate, but never that I'd resist. And she doesn't understand why, which makes me angriest.

When she joins the Matron and they look at me as if I'm pitiful, I understand I won't be given a choice. How much agency did I think I'd be given traveling with a group of missionaries?

Scarlet is everywhere. The ink in my journal when I try to write. The holy relics' garments when I spy them huddled against me. When it spreads across the floor—like a spilled bucket of blood inching toward my cot—I rub my eyes to dispel the visions.

Exhaustion falls over me like a veil. I yawn without covering my mouth.

I ball up a fist again just to feel my fingernails bite into the softness of my palm. When I slam it into the mattress, my knuckles brush my journal. A corner of paper sticks out from the spine. Glancing around, I draw it out and recognize it as the letter the writer gave me at our parting. There was so much excitement and rushing around, I'd completely forgotten it!

I unfold it carefully and spread it over my skirt, smoothing its creases.

It begins, *Dear Quite Contrary*.

This brings a rare smile out of me.

From what I have gleaned of yourself and your companions in the short time we were acquainted, I think you must be crawling the walls by now.

I nearly laugh aloud.

I have but one message to pass to you, knowledge that I can offer, that I myself wish I had known when I was younger. Our differences are not our strengths. They are not weaknesses either, though they can and will be disadvantageous. They are simply who we are.

Do not let anyone tear you down because of your differences, but beware any pedestal they offer up as well, because it is never well intentioned. When I was a boy, I wished for nothing so much as to simply be like others—so much so that I accepted the attention without examining the intention.

I suppose this is a fancy way of saying, always be undeniably you. And be aware when others are trying to dictate to you who that is.

That is how your garden grows.

~ ~ ~

I tear up. I'm not certain what I'm feeling: frustration, sadness, or even understanding. I need to get away from this place.

Jack is watching me from the shadows of the narrow stone stairs. He's become such a fixture, no one pays him any mind anymore. He leans against the wall until he knows he has my attention. He stretches his mouth wider than mine and flexes his gloved hands like a tiger's paws. I stifle a much-needed laugh. He pantomimes the sun going down, my companions going to sleep, and the two of us creeping out of the church.

Is he joking? He raises his eyebrows questioningly, maybe daringly. Then he's gone.

I long to escape this stifling antagonism. And the terror of being judged for the jarring noises I make. On that matter, I cannot back down.

But who is this Jack? Not like any friend I've had before. An English boy. It makes no difference to me if he's not high-born. But can he be trusted? I never doubted that with Nancy, Sally, or even puffed-up Sarah Hillman.

I'm so far from home. Mama would tie me down rather than have me go with him. Reverend Lee would urge caution. But Beatrice would tell me to do anything to flee the holy relics' grasp. Every time I think of her, I feel the sting of my betrayal. By coming here, I took these crusaders' side against her. And I am wondering if I will receive what I was promised in turn.

I put on my stiff nightgown and mobcap over my clothes. I lie on my cot among the others. I cannot hear their breathing or snoring. But I can see when they are no longer restless and their bodies relax with sleep.

Since I only mean to go on a lark with Jack, I leave my possessions behind, along with a brief note for Miss Mitchell. I am here by her grace and don't want her to worry. Surely, they'll be so consumed by their ongoing struggle with Dr. Watson, they will barely notice I'm gone. At least, that's what I tell her—and myself.

Jack is waiting where he said he'd be. A half-moon keeps us obscured but I can still read his vivid face. I follow his cue and walk as if all is normal. My humble clothes match his dress, so we could be taken for siblings. London is a city of dreams, and I'm not certain I'm wakeful as I follow his lead over untold streets.

Chapter Twenty-Six

The air on the bank of the Thames is chilly for spring, and I press my shawl around my shoulders. During the day, sailboats go back and forth, carrying imported goods to various markets. At night, the larger boats are docked by the bank while smaller ferries and rowboats move across the rushing water. In the distance, I feel a big clock chime midnight.

Small cook fires dot the dark shoreline, with groups of people gathered around them. Jack gestures and I follow down a set of damp stone steps to a narrow wharf. I watched him put his fingers in his mouth, and the sound he makes must be shrill, because I feel it in my back teeth. We wait a moment until a waterman steers toward us, his thick arms masterfully working his oar and rudder.

The vessel is flat and broad with a rope border that is presumably meant to keep one from falling in the drink, though Jack slips under it without trouble. He and the waterman greet each other with friendly familiarity. He gestures at me as I board. I can tell he's spinning a yarn, a real whale of a tale. He doesn't realize I have a teacher's instincts for foolery. I'll play along while it suits me, but he won't get the best of me.

Jack sits on the plain wood, and I follow suit, folding my legs underneath me. As the waterman pushes away from shore with his oar, a girl appears, waving her arms. She jumps the widening gap, over the water and onto the ferry until she is beside us, grinning. She has a friendly gap between her two front teeth and one of the prettiest faces I've ever seen. Her black freckles on tan skin remind me of Sally.

She says something to me, and I see Jack intercept, explaining. When she looks at me, I can tell she is forcing the words from her mouth slowly and loudly. I grimace unconsciously, and Jack frowns and makes a motion with his hands. His message of *don't do that* is clear. She nods, unbothered, and smiles at me in apology.

With a quill she keeps in her skirts, she clumsily scratches a word into the wood of the ferry. I tilt my head to read it. The letters are large and uneven. She must not have much more schooling than Jack does.

Dot, I read. She jerks her thumb at herself, and I score my name too.

The river is fast and a bit rough, but the waterman navigates it deftly. I watch the people we pass on the bank, squinting against the darkness. I see a lone soldier standing there, and a shiver runs up my spine. Is this my writer friend's ghostly soldier come to bring me an omen? A lady grabs his hand, and suddenly he is laughing and turns away. I see other redcoats join them and the spell is broken.

Jack nudges me. He opens his mouth and then purses it in thought. He spreads his hands out as if he's running them over the surface of the water. Tunneling his head down, his countenance changes as if he is troubled and uncomfortable. He blows into his hands. He is cold. He is freezing. He points at the water again and knocks a fist against the solid wood. I don't like pantomime. It usually comes off as insulting. But like Ezra Brewer, Jack is a natural storyteller.

Raising my eyebrows in question, I put my arms up against my body and shiver. He nods, looking gleeful that I understand. I can't imagine the river freezing over. Does it turn purely solid? Do people traverse it like a road?

He claps his hands in time, creating a rhythm I can feel as I sit beside him. Dot gets up and does a small dance, which earns us scorn from the waterman when the ferry begins to tip back and forth. Are they telling me there's a party on the ice?

Before I can try to question them, I feel the ferry bump against the embankment, where other barges transport goods or passengers. Dot says goodbye to us and slips away with a word to Jack.

We jump ashore and make our way through bales of wool that make me homesick. We pass crates of vegetables and sacks of grain. Are we headed to a market? I'd like to see how it compares to Faneuil Hall in Boston. This is a rare exploratory mission I'm not likely to get from the relics, or maybe ever again.

We wind our way through the dark and emerge onto a thoroughfare. In the dim gaslight, I read the signs on the storefronts. So many coffee and tea shops! The one closest to us reads *Twinings*, and a wonderful lingering fragrance emanates from it. I recognize it as Earl Grey! How I've missed tea times with Mama, which no doubt the relics would find frivolous.

Farther down, I see a handful of printshops. I glance around in wonder, dreaming for a moment of my scribbles run off and given out to the public. What would that be like, to be a known writer? Perhaps like my friend from the crossing. I will have to come up with a man's pen name, as I certainly couldn't publish under my own. Before any come to mind, Jack urges me on. He is bossier than Liam, but with similar gumption. I stifle my amusement.

We slip through an alley and across a few darker streets until finally we emerge into an open market filled with shacks and stalls. This must be Covent Garden! Miss Mitchell had uncharitable things to say about it and the people here as I presumed she would about fancy ladies with faces painted to exaggeration. We pass a merchant who claims to sell fresh fish, but the smell says otherwise. My diet has been genuinely disgusting since I embarked on this voyage, such a contrast to the Vineyard, with its bounty of daily fishing and farming.

I start when Jack bumps into a man and apologizes

profusely. The man raises his hand as if to strike him but then just grumbles and walks away. Jack grins as he leads me to a stall, where he removes a leather wallet from the breast of his frock coat. I cock an eyebrow at him. A little pickpocket, eh? Shamefully, I don't demand he give it back. I don't want Jack to know I see through him yet.

He pays the merchant, and she hands over a few hard, opaque white sticks. Jack puts one in his mouth and sucks. I give mine an experimental lick. Pure sugar, melted, cooled, and twisted into this magical treat I'm tasting.

We stroll together, perusing the shops. I marvel at a small display of fireworks, the orange flare blinding me momentarily as the men light them and then run to safety. Jack looks content. He's in his element. Why do I have such a soft spot for the misfits?

Is this what it's like when they hold a fair on the ice after a freeze? I wonder if that's why he told me that story. There are so many things to see, smell, and touch—I almost lose myself in my senses for a moment.

I pet an old shaggy dog that's searching for supper on the ground, and he tries to snatch the hard candy from my mouth. I pull away, laughing. Jack's eyes twinkle at my delight.

I notice that, while we meander, he does so with purpose. He's sneakier than Reverend Lee was in taking me to the Tisbury parish, but if I can help it, I won't be tricked again.

When we arrive at a grand building with lovely colonnades flanking its front, Jack takes me around the back to the shadows of an alley. Letters painted on an old building read: *Stage Door*. I see him whistle again and then give the door a series of timed knocks.

The door cracks open and Dot's pleasing face appears. She grins as he hands her a hard candy before stepping aside to let us in.

We are backstage among the ropes and platforms the stagehands use. Jack puts his hand on a knotted ladder hanging from the scaffolding and raises his brow at me. Can I climb? With a sniff, I push him away with the back of my hand and take hold of the rope. I scaled trees with ease when I was younger. I boarded a ship with a treacherous ladder. I am much more adept than he'd expected.

He climbs a rope beside me and shows me how to

slide on my belly to the wooden platform dangling above and alongside the stage. From up here, I see a good deal of the enraptured audience. The actors step in and out of my view as they come to the front of the stage. Jack folds his hands and rests his chin on them, watching and listening. He finally seems as young as I estimated him to be.

A grand actress appears to wash her hands in a feverish manner, and I challenge myself to guess the play. It's *Macbeth*! Jack is transfixed by this cruel lady's remorse as she attempts to clean off invisible blood, a sign of her guilt.

When my companion shakes his head as if to clear his mind, I understand we must leave before the end. But at least I got to glimpse a late-night production at a real London theater, a far more dazzling spectacle than the occasional theatrics in the Chilmark Meeting House.

Dot holds my waist to keep me from slipping as we make our way down the ropes. When I turn to face her, she has a worried expression. Having no other means to inquire about her well-being, I let my eyes droop and turn down the corners of my mouth. She steps back, showing great concern. Is she afraid? A shadow of doubt creeps into me.

Jack witnesses the last part of our exchange. He jumps down, casts a fierce glance at Dot, and breaks into an amusing grimace, his eyes popping out. But I don't laugh with him. Something about his and Dot's conflicting expressions gives me pause. He must realize I'm suspicious and points to a nearby wall that features two masks side by side, one comic, one tragic.

I nod to acknowledge that great stories contain elements of humor and sadness, often in equal amounts. Though the scales of fate sometimes seem to favor one over the other. If one is glad or hurt, it's easy to forget the opposite exists. Thinking about how all of this is contained in the plays and players of a grand theater makes me want to see more!

I give a small curtsy to thank Dot for the magical experience, until Jack whisks me away, no doubt with the next destination in mind. I'm still deciding how much farther I'll let him lead me astray without calling his bluff.

We walk leisurely rather than at my companion's usual frantic pace. This may have to do with Jack pantomiming, fluffing a pillow under his head and comically yawning, which turns into the real thing. I rub my eyes, and my mouth stretches open involuntarily too.

I notice we're not returning the way we came. I will not be able to sneak back into the missionaries' lodgings before they awake to read my note. I feel a pang of remorse mixed with leftover anger. This will likely be my last bit of freedom in London—remarkable details to add to my journal. I don't protest.

We move away from the brightest lights and follow narrower, winding streets, which are frankly unclean. I don't mean to judge Jack's home. The Covent Garden crowd would certainly turn up their noses at my modest island sheep farm.

I thought we'd stop at a snug hovel. I imagined Jack's mother greeting us, and gently boxing his ears for coming in late, before she offered us a plate of stew and split up what coppers he'd made for the day. Despite his appearance of being carefree, it's obvious he's not on his own. Someone helped him present himself for the job of courier.

A man meets Jack at the door as we're about to

enter. Despite looking like a ruddy Englishman with a funny hat, he has elegant digits. They feel slippery as he takes my hand, and I decide to call him Mr. Fingers. He reaches into his pocket and gives Jack a shiny coin that he tosses in the air. What did he do to earn it?

As we climb the stairs in a dilapidated building, a full-body shiver runs through me. I see Jack slip the money into his coat pocket, which suddenly takes on the appearance of hot coals. His jacket is burning—the flames climb up his arm. Mr. Fingers seems to be made of leaves that are ablaze! I shouldn't have come this far.

The wind swings the door open below us. It creates a momentary distraction. I slide down the crumbling banister, fall to the rickety floor, and I'm out of that den of tods as quick as a vixen! But Jack gives chase.

I become furious when I realize he was trading me for silver! How much was I worth? Would I wind up as free labor in a place like the "school" for the blind? Nothing about Jack is humorous anymore. How foolish I was to think I could get the better of him!

I run for safety. But the crafty fiend is gaining on me! I gasp when someone clutches my elbow. I turn to see Dot's attentive face. It's obvious from her expression that while she was initially privy to the scheme, she couldn't go through with it. She's aiding me out in the open now, with who knows how many confederates on watch.

Her courage shames me, reminding me how I turned away from Beatrice when I too could have shown courage by not signing on with missionaries. What were her last words that Thomas signed? "Remember the shoals!" Know when to run and give it your all.

Dot has a map of this city in her head, and she moves ably by my side. I can almost feel the tide rushing at the back of my feet, but never catching up. We leave Jack in the dust.

We spend an hour or so peering into store windows and visiting the city's central stables. The horses and riders are preparing for another busy day. Dot and I stroke the muzzles of several proud beasts and sit upright pretending to powder our noses in the fanciest of carriages before we're chased out.

Dot is determined to see me safely back to the church. As I am wondering how much trouble I'm in, a faded poster in a storefront window catches my eye. It reads, *You are welcome to attend a lecture by Abbé Sicard. Learn about his noble pursuits and witness the hand language he uses to communicate with deaf-mutes at his school in Paris.*

It is dated six days ago, while we were languishing nearby. But at last, here is the means for me to move us forward. There's not a moment to lose!

Chapter Twenty-Seven

Around dawn, Dot and I locate the church where the relics and I are lodging. As we approach, I notice Chestnuts standing guard at street level. When she sees me, she rushes down the stairs, presumably to alert the others.

Dot recedes even as I shake my head and point to her and then our lodgings. I pat my chest above my heart to express my gratitude and tell her I will share the story of her heroism with my companions. She rubs her cheek and laughs.

She lifts her hands in the air and turns around. London is her city. I want to spare her any dire consequences for helping me. She crosses her arms and looks at me before pointing to a bakery a few doors down.

I raise my hand to indicate for her to wait as Miss Mitchell hurries to greet me. She holds me by the shoulders, looks me up and down, and squeezes me in a surprising embrace. Does she truly care for me? I smile and nod to indicate that I'm fine.

Before I give any explanation for my absence, I pull Miss Mitchell toward the bakery. She doesn't resist. She must think I'm very hungry, and I suppose I am. I ask for two rolls, which are warm and soft between my hands.

When we return, I put one in Dot's hands. She inhales it with eyes closed, then takes a nibble. While Miss Mitchell and the others surround me, Dot expertly slips away.

All eyes peer at me. I read concern, curiosity, disapproval, perhaps envy. That nasty Freckles! Thank goodness, Miss Mitchell puts her arm around my shoulders and gently leads me down the stairs to our basement room. She gestures for me to wash at the basin. I feel so grimy, I wish I could bathe in the sea.

Afterward, I sit on my cot. I must sigh audibly as I remove my boots and massage my feet. Everyone has followed. Are there tears in Miss Mitchell's eyes? I feel great remorse.

It's the Matron who takes up paper and pen. Her writing is large and demanding. It appears no deception is necessary. She has written, *Where can we find that ungodly boy?*

Who? I stupidly write, and I can see her snort.

The ragamuffin who kidnapped you. That's how it happened, right?

I spell "yes" with my hands. That's my first instinct. Luckily, I'm not understood. I have time to move my hands while my mind slows down. I need to think quickly but say what's right.

I can't go over every moment since Jack and I met to judge if he was ever sincere. When he chased me through the streets, did he have a change of heart? Could Jack the artful have (briefly) become Jack the good? I'd like to think so. Can a child be held responsible for wickedness if it is abetted or even directed by an indecent, nay criminal, adult? I find I'm most worried about his safety.

I'd have that repulsive Mr. Fingers in chains if I could! But where would Jack and the other orphan boys in that rundown boardinghouse go? At least they have one another. And they're free in a city that's made them who they are—someone I'll never be, with the privilege of choosing my travels and returning to a loving home.

I write to Miss Mitchell, *I was distressed and felt*

trapped by Dr. Watson's indecisions and demands. The boy showed me the sights, but he didn't drag me away. I know it may be impossible for you to understand . . .

Miss Mitchell stops my hands and takes the journal.

The Matron has told Dr. Watson we are finished here and will not recommend his asylum to missions who follow our path.

I'm so relieved, I break into uncontrollable laughter. Before they suggest the next course of action, I write what I saw on the poster.

The relics look at one another and me in disbelief. I implore Miss Mitchell to inquire if there's any chance Abbé Sicard is still in London. But, in any case, it's time we headed to his esteemed school in Paris, where we have a better chance of being welcomed.

The relics insist that I wash all my garments, and I am more than happy to oblige. After I hang the clothes to dry, the Matron instructs me to pray and go to sleep lest I catch a fever from my unexpected adventure. The basement is so cold that I've been sleeping in full garb the past week. Now I have no such luxury. As I lie shivering under a thin blanket in nothing but a shift, I can't help but feel I'm doing penance.

I try to imagine a Frenchman who is fluent in a different sign language and pray he is not a myth. For months, I've had to suffer the relics' constant slights and aggressions, only to be dismayed by the actions of instructors who appear self-interested. I hold out a final hope there's a place where deaf children can live safely and receive the education they deserve. If not, all my efforts have been wasted.

Part Three

France

Chapter Twenty-Eight

We successfully cross the Channel from England to France. I unloose my hair, let it blow in the wind, and feel the sea spray on my face. The Matron speaks rapidly, her mouth flapping like a carp. I don't let her spoil my fun, and when she tries to pull Miss Mitchell into the scold, she waves her hand, seeming to say, *Let her be*. Freckles might like to toss off her bonnet, but she affects utmost piousness to make me look bad.

Chestnuts, on the other hand, gives me a shy smile and turns her face to the wan shadow of the sun. I wonder what she could be if she was not always pulling back in deference to her sister.

At my urging, Miss Mitchell found an Englishman who had attended Abbé Sicard's speech and discovered that he had left London to return to his duties at the Paris school. The man was complimentary to the abbé. Miss Mitchell then sent word that we would stop to visit for instruction during our journey. Sicard is presently awaiting us. My heart beats out of my chest at the thought of meeting this self-possessed hearing teacher who is dedicated to giving the deaf opportunities that they would not otherwise have in the outside world. Many former students are teachers at the school.

My hand shakes with excitement as I record this in my journal, while we await transportation to the Paris school. Miss Mitchell speaks to the Matron, who heaves a great sigh. She appears to agree with whatever Miss Mitchell has communicated.

Miss Mitchell then gestures for me to sit next to her on a bench and instinctively makes the sign for writing. I turn to a clean page and hand her my journal, turning it upside down and backward.

Mary, I have been reflecting on our experiences in London.

I wait for her to write more, curious what will follow.

Regarding what I've said of Dr. Watson's character and motives, it is my most earnest and particular request that no publicity be given, in any form. Each of us has the right to form our own opinion. But it's important to consider what we say openly about others.

This might be the most decent thing she's said to

me. I nod, promising to keep silent on the subject. I hope she'll extend the same good form to our French hosts. She has hinted at her disgust for Catholics.

When our carriage finally arrives, we board and settle in. I peer at the passing sights. It's starting to lightly rain, and the lush green countryside looks vibrant. I try to turn back but in this weather I can't see the White Cliffs of Dover, where we started our trip on the England side. A thin gray mist clings to the air above the water.

Looking out over the flat, lush landscape that stretches to the beaches and then the sea makes my heart long for my modest sheep farm.

It is a long trip from Calais to Paris. I close my eyes, wishing for success in my efforts. I must doze because when I am nudged awake by Miss Mitchell, I don't feel the clomp, clomp of the horses anymore.

A stately building with multiple stories made of smooth stone sprawls before us. Greenery tumbles from the wrought-iron grates. The lawns are extensive and beautifully manicured. We are greeted by a young, hearing assistant with quick eyes and nimble hands whom I'll call the Interpreter. When Miss Mitchell explains to her who we are, we are welcomed warmly and immediately taken to see the head of the school. Quite a difference from the asylum in London, where only the Matron was granted audience after a lengthy negotiation. At last, we shall meet Abbé Sicard. Even the Matron is at a loss for words!

I wipe my perspiring palms on my skirt. I have rarely been this eager to make a good first impression.

Abbé Sicard sits at a magisterial desk, with the relics and me seated in front of him. He is an old man, slightly hunched but still impressive in the attention his presence commands. His white hair is combed neatly with a slight flip at its end; a small silk skullcap adorns the crown of his head. He appears solemn, as men of the church usually are, but he has a cherubic mouth that looks as if it is quick to smile. His sign language is indeed fascinating and quite different from our style on the Vineyard.

There is a blackboard in his office for him to write on when others don't know French sign language. None of this is unusual to me—except he writes in French, which I cannot read.

Luckily, Chestnuts—I am *finally* introduced to her

by her Christian name, Helene—is fluent in his native language. She springs to action as interpreter.

The Matron asks the abbé if he is the founder of this school. He signs directly to me as he speaks to the relics, but I understand none of it, so I too am reliant on Helene's translated words on the blackboard. The conversation progresses in stops and starts, while each party waits for a translation, and then for their message to be conveyed.

I am used to this form of communication. The relics, however, quickly grow impatient. I worry their facial expressions convey rudeness.

No, no. Charles-Michel de l'Épée was the founder of this remarkable institution. I learned a lot from him, and I succeeded him after his death. He is much revered by all, though the methods we use today are different from his.

My fingers flex with questions, but before I can venture to ask, Miss Mitchell speaks. Helene assists the abbé in understanding with his limited English.

How did Abbé de l'Épée become interested in the education of the deaf?

Abbé Sicard seems pleased to recall his predecessor's history. He settles back in his chair and folds his hands over his stomach before beginning to speak again. I lean forward unconsciously, with rapt interest.

There is a most interesting account I'll share with you. Initially, Abbé de l'Épée was interested in charitable services for the poor. He had occasion to call at a house in Paris. The mother was not at home, and while he was waiting for her, he spoke to her two young daughters; but their eyes remained fixed on their work, and they gave no answer. In vain did he renew his questions; they were silent again. He knew not that those whom he addressed were created by nature never to hear nor speak. The mother came in, and everything was explained.

I finally have a moment for inquiry. I sign first to demonstrate with pride my Vineyard language. Abbé Sicard watches me with fascination. Not as though I'm a curiosity, but rather a missing piece in the puzzle of deaf communication and education, which obsesses us both. I write on the board.

How did he initially attempt to teach them, and how have the methods changed since?

The abbé stands as if he has a pressing engagement. I watch closely as he signs to me. Chestnuts, I mean Helene, conveys his spoken response.

A fine question! You will find out in time. I extend an invitation for your group to take instruction at the school, beginning with the most basic lessons. Now, please excuse me, mesdemoiselles.

I am elated beyond words. But I sense a dissatisfaction among my companions. Except for Helene, who seems to share my exhilaration. I can't imagine why she joined the holy relics. It's possible, despite her religious training and vows, she's never played such a useful role. Before we arrived here, I would have mistaken her for her sister's shadow if not for the few smiles she's dared give me.

Her smile fades now as the Matron turns to her, speaking sharply.

Helene begins transcribing again. *I translated in writing rather than speech so all could understand. I assumed you wouldn't mind reading. I'm sorry if—*

The Matron forcibly takes the chalk from her hand. Shocked, I look at Miss Mitchell, whose eyes are flashing. They talk to Helene, completely shutting me out. Her own sister stands back with tight lips, not defending her. This is no surprise. Helene must have crossed an invisible barrier by stepping out of her place as shy and unassuming. I wave my hand in an attempt to thank her for her assistance. She's been very brave, and I want to show her my support.

It's clear the holy relics are not in charge anymore. The Paris school is a place for me, and people like me. I take another piece of chalk from the board and write for all in the room to see. *You have gotten a taste of how deaf people navigate an unaccommodating world.*

There's an ugliness in the Matron and Miss Mitchell I have not seen before. It does not come from injustice but personal hurt. They're glimpsing an inkling now of how I have felt the entire way here, how I've been treated—with rare exception. It must be eye-opening to be part of a conversation you don't understand. Will they simmer down? Otherwise, their whole mission—to aid unfortunate souls who lack hearing—is in doubt.

Chapter Twenty-Nine

After we leave the abbé's office, my companions seem to find their bearings again. The Interpreter who met us at the door—she is fluent in French and French sign language—leads us around the campus. We're all agog. In different ways.

The school is enormous, with long, narrow hallways and steep, narrow stairs we climb in single file. The wooden floors are scuffed from many feet shuffling along them, and the whitewashed walls are lined along the bottom with dark paneling. I believe the woman is describing large gardens in the back. I can't wait to see it all!

Students are walking all around us. We get some curious glances, but most of them speak among themselves, their hands moving deftly, confidently. They talk and tease and flirt and laugh, like my class back home, but better behaved! They are primly uniformed, but each has put a personal touch to their outfit. They are disciplined but don't seem demure or intimidated.

Is this what the relics expected? If I were to guess, I'd imagine their idea of helping the deaf is more like Abbé de l'Épée's—the thrill of coming across two daughters without language in a poor home. Here the deaf are organized and social. I hope this is the environment the Matron and her league seek to foster when they travel farther east.

A girl meets me at the entrance of the dormitory. She appears to be about eight years old and wears the pinafore uniform I've observed on the younger children. She looks like a pixie, a slip of a thing with a huge bow. She sweetly curtsies and gestures to me alone. For the first night since the voyage, I will not have to sleep with the relics. I'll stay in a girls' dormitory.

I look back at my traveling companions, who stand with the Interpreter. I do not know where they will be lodging. They don't look displeased, but I can tell Miss Mitchell is sorry to be separated from me. Before she departs, she gently hugs herself—a warm message for me. I do hope our purposes here in Paris will align.

The pale little sprite with the large bow runs me up three flights of stairs, clutching my hand like I'm her dolly.

The room has four beds on either side with large windows letting in light. It is sanitary but not impersonal. I walk toward the freshly made bed where my trunk has been kindly deposited at the footboard.

I am surrounded by girls all younger than me, whose hands are flying, asking me dozens of questions I can't understand. When I introduce myself in Vineyard sign, they look at one another with wide eyes, then break into laughter. Oh dear! Have I said something funny or rude in French sign language?

One girl with sleek black hair points to me, urging me to sign more. I do so animatedly so that we may learn one another's languages—or meet somewhere in the middle—like Bill and me at the London asylum.

Now the girls are near hysteria. Surely, I cannot have spoken impolitely to them at every turn. They're teasing me, which makes me cross. I am already conscious of my age, size, and dowdy attire compared with them. Before I snap back, I remind myself I am here to learn to be a better teacher.

It would never have occurred to me that a group of deaf people would find their sign language superior to any other. I imagine Ezra Brewer twisting his wrist in a mock-fancy fashion to indicate French people. It lifts my mood.

But I don't think these girls are snobby or unkind. Everything is silly at a certain age. If they don't gang up and tie me down, I'll be glad for the sprites' camaraderie and spark of life. And I will show them. I'll learn their language and maybe teach them something in the process!

As I slowly unpack my trunk, a girl approaches. She's more amiable than the others, with a glowing round face and dimples. I can read her expression. She's sheepish about her friends' behavior. She spells her name in the bewitching one-handed alphabet. I spell mine with two hands. Then she makes a twisting motion next to the right side of her head to indicate her lovely blonde curls.

I understand! I cradle the right side of my face in my right palm, the nickname Papa gave me as an infant. She must have had a curl as a baby. This type of name sign is obviously a familiar deaf tradition on both sides of the Atlantic. After all, it takes time to keep spelling names. Now we know each other a little bit.

I nod at her. She points at my pillow, where an object rests.

I seize it and press it to my lips. A letter from Mama! All the way here in Paris.

The girl seems to understand and leaves me alone to sit on my bed and read it.

> My dearest Mary,
>
> I feel your absence so keenly and pray—even as I'm doing my daily chores—that you are safe. The idea of you traversing the globe is still unreal to me after all these months.
>
> Papa has become quieter, and the house would feel hollow if it were not for your (and now our) friend Nora. She brings such enthusiasm, but also respect to the task of learning our signs and engaging townsfolk to assist her.
>
> This isn't the sort of story I'd usually share, but she came across Mrs. Butler signing with Mrs. Hillman on the high road and inquired why they were talking with their hands when they had the ability of speech. They admitted they were gossiping about a neighbor who bent over to tend tomatoes and split her skirt.
>
> They thought it was less rude to mention the anecdote in signs.

You know how it is, but Nora was tickled pink!

She is a fine cook and laundress, but I miss you boiling the milk and leaving a hot iron on the linens.

Nora has become friendly with Eamon, and she is very stern but loving with the boys.

I haven't returned to church since we walked out together. The Pyes and my guide Reverend Lee invite us to supper and we return the favor.

I've been planting a garden. I hope it will be in bloom when you come home.

You _must_ return.

Please reply when you receive this in Paris so I will know you have safely arrived. Mrs. Pye's brother-in-law, Daniel Trees, promised to keep it dry in his coat pocket and return with your letter. He's docking in France and spending time in Paris for several weeks.

I'm sure you are filling your journal. I can't wait to hear of your adventures—the ones that won't make me tear out my hair!

My wise, passionate, obstinate, fearless daughter—never forget us.

All my love,
Mama

I try to hide my tears. Missing Mama and Papa squeezes my heart and makes it difficult to breathe—but I have just begun here. Will I always feel torn in half?

As I gently refold the letter, something falls out of the envelope. It's a short note on a slip of paper. I recognize the handwriting as Liam's.

> Miss Mary,
>
> We had a dance in the barn. We sang in Irish. The dirt shook under our feet as we stomped in line. Yellow Leg caught a fat rat. A fine gift!

An image of the sad and happy masks at Covent Garden flashes in my mind—the boy brings the joy.

Chapter Thirty

We wake early. I'm relieved to see new clothes draped over my trunk. But I groan when I realize I'll be wearing a frock with puffy sleeves, a pinafore, and stockings. Even if it's a tidy uniform, I feel childish. Then I realize if they have one in my size, there must be older students here dressed in similar fashion.

I don't know if Little Curls intervened, but the other girls don't think I'm humorous this morning. They seem to accept my presence. We file down to a dining hall to eat a simple breakfast of porridge with fresh berries. It's amazing to see so many hands signing grace. I am uplifted! For the first time since I've left home, I feel like a fresh bud on a tree. I am starting my education anew.

Little Curls makes sure I find my classroom. I'd nearly forgotten that Abbé Sicard invited us all to take a beginner's course until I see the Matron, Miss Mitchell, Helene, and Freckles in the room. They look more incongruous with these young pupils than

I do. But at least they're not wearing pinafores!

As a teacher, I believe it's never too late to learn. But how will they take the instruction? Will they be open to learning sign (and making mistakes, as all new learners do) among deaf pupils?

I can't help but wonder if this is part of the Second Great Reawakening, an outpouring of religious fervor, that Miss Mitchell described when we first met. I wave to her, and she seems excited to see me. Is the Paris school working its magic on her too?

As soon as the Matron scolds her with a sour look from a few rows behind, the moment is lost.

I've positioned myself close to the front so I can see all. The lesson commences and I am mesmerized by the instructor, who has wispy reddish hair, a slim mouth, and a fantastical Roman nose. He appears somewhat eccentric in his ill-fitting coat with several watches draping his left arm. His signing is both sophisticated and simple. The mark of a great orator. I can intuit his meaning even if I don't understand his language.

I sense movement at the back of the room, and Helene comes forward with the Interpreter. It appears the Interpreter will speak in French what the instructor signs, and then Helene will translate into English on the chalkboard. Disappointingly, Freckles, the Matron, and Miss Mitchell don't move up to read it easily.

The teacher explains something with great charm, and the children look eager to play along. The Interpreter whispers to Helene and she writes, *Let's show our new friends how to sign the ABCs.*

Fortunately, both English and French use the Latin, or Roman, alphabet, so I recognize the letters on the board.

A is simple. A closed hand with the thumb tucked at the side.

B is a little trickier. You hold up one hand, left or right. Four fingers are held together, and you tuck your thumb into your palm.

C is obvious. It looks like you've curved your four fingers and thumb into the shape of the letter.

ABC...

The teacher quickly skips back, making a "b hand," touching the tips of his fingers to his chin, then bringing that hand down into his other open palm. Soon, all the children are doing the same.

The woman whispers to Helene. Her face lights up. She writes, *Bon! That means "good" in French, and you make the sign using your "b hand."*

Soon, the pupils are signing "good day" to me and the missionaries. The sign for "day" resembles what we use on the Vineyard, indicating the sun's passage from dawn to dusk.

This little lesson serves as a key. As we continue, I begin to unlock the unique style of French sign language. I am so rapt I hardly notice time passing. I want to learn more and more!

When most of the others have gotten up to leave, Helene touches my shoulder gently. I stayed behind to meet the instructor, but he is gone. Helene slowly finger-spells his name, Jean Massieu.

The rest of our traveling group joins us at the front of the room. Miss Mitchell immediately resorts to writing on a slate rather than practicing what we learned. *I've missed you! It looked like you were quickly catching on to the lesson. I'm afraid I'm a little slower.*

I smile and shake my head to let her know speed is not of the essence.

She continues. *I will ask Abbé Sicard if we can have*

a small instructional group to teach us the basics we need for our purposes. After all, we are missionaries, not sign language instructors.

The Matron, who is reading her words, nods vigorously.

I write, *I think I can learn quickly. I believe our agreement was that I would come as far as Paris and help you in gaining entrance to establishments such as this. I'm not to go farther east with you. I don't know who was assigned to take me back to America, but I certainly want to spend at least a month here.*

Miss Mitchell writes, *Because of our lack of success in England, we'd like you to continue on a bit farther with us. We'll stay here another week. Seven more girls from the league will arrive in Paris by then.*

I'm taken aback and don't know what to say. I glimpse Helene out of the corner of my eye. She's wringing her hands and looks distressed. When did they decide to change their plans—and the course of my life?

Since I'm here by their grace, I realize I will have to find deaf advocates at the highest level, and quickly.

Before I can scheme, Little Curls runs back into

the room. I can tell she's looking for me, and I gladly raise my hand above my head to motion her over. When she reaches our group and signs to me with excitement, she receives rude looks in return.

I nod enthusiastically, as if I understand all she's telling me. Miss Mitchell writes me a message, but I let my classmate whisk me away, shrugging as if I don't have a choice. I hope her plans will take me away from the relics' grasp, at least temporarily.

Miss Mitchell's words play themselves over in my mind. "We'd like you to continue on a bit farther with us." Beatrice warned me of this exact situation. If I don't contrive a plan to hold them to their promise, could I be stuck with them for years and years?

Chapter Thirty-One

Little Curls leads me to the garden, tugging me spiritedly by the arm. I follow willingly, dispelling the shadow the relics have cast over me. How can I leave this place when I've only just arrived and begun to glimpse its riches?

It is a brilliant, sunny day. The lawns are bright green in the sunshine, the hedges trim and sculpted. We follow pathways of laid stone. I imagine a palace having a garden such as this. Recalling the small garden Mama planted for my return brings a lump to my throat.

Around us, students stand together in groups, their fingers flying as they talk and laugh and gossip. Some are my age, some older. The younger ones are playing: one group with pickup sticks, another a game I would call ninepin. They've set up nine small pillars and throw a ball at them, trying to knock over the most in one toss.

Little Curls sits me down on a bench and removes

from her pocket a paper disc with a string attached to either side. On the front is a lovely illustration of a bird, a bright red cardinal. She turns the disc over, revealing a picture of an upside-down cage. As she pulls the string tight on both sides and rubs it back and forth between her fingers, the disc in the middle spins. I gasp! In a flash, it appears the bird is in the cage—an optical illusion!

I must frown because she stops and looks at me with a quizzical gaze. "What?" she signs.

I make the sign for a flying bird, then fold its wings and trap it. I'm feeling too sympathetic to the cardinal at the moment. She looks upset. I smile quickly and nod to tell her I like the trick.

She cocks her head slightly as she examines me. "Your mama?" she asks, lifting her eyebrows.

Is she referring to the letter I received? I indicate a great distance, then a basic dwelling, filling in some details like our barn, sheep, and farm dog. She looks puzzled. I would think these signs are nearly universal, but she has something else on her mind.

She points to yellow blooms and then twists her fingers like making a braid. She crowns herself with it, her face making a pompous expression. I burst out laughing.

"Miss Mitchell?" I finger-spell, trying to remember as much of the French alphabet as I can. I suppose we've just given her a name sign with the hair crown. I laugh again, and it feels so good, as if exhaling for the first time after holding my breath for too long.

No flames or burning figures blur my vision; the only wall around me is a garden.

Little Curls crosses her eyes and imitates Miss Mitchell signing the French alphabet with poorly shaped letters, hand facing in so others can't read them. This only sets me off harder until I'm wiping tears from my eyes. I shake my head. "Travel with. Mama is at home."

I notice when I sign, she imitates the movements in her lap. Am I so interesting compared to what she knows? Does she see me the way I see her, a different way to be what and who we are?

Other girls are drawn toward us, their eyes curious and bright. One begins to tell a story, and I recognize only a few words here and there. Still, I am engrossed in the telling.

Even when I don't understand, I don't feel left out. I am not like Miss Mitchell. I'm not used to the outside world always bending to me. And besides, these girls want to include me.

I repeat the signs I don't comprehend. They use letters and gestures to explain until I grasp them. Then they eagerly wait for me to show them Vineyard signs. They grin at the differences but try to memorize them or find a connection, as I do. I feel my defenses as an outsider slipping away. I'm being drawn into the circle. With this level of immersion, we can learn quickly together.

"Maison" is fancier than "house."

"Mademoiselle" is grander than "girl."

"Étoile" is so much lovelier than "star"!

They seem captivated by my description of Ezra Brewer and my account of us being chased on the high seas by Andrew Noble. I give myself shivers!

An older girl with long hair and a lovely beauty

mark on her cheek tells me her name is Anne—and shows me her name sign by making a dot on her face with her pinky. She and her friend Rosalie—with glossy hair like a raven's wing—urge me to the makeshift ninepin court. Little Curls follows, holding my hand. I take my turns tossing the ball, watching it streak against the slick grass and miss the wooden pins every time.

I don't worry that I'm being spoken to when turned the other way, or that someone will get cross with me for not understanding them. After many months, I feel as if my shoulders are finally unknotting. My face is relaxed and grinning. My hands aren't balled up and speechless.

It's unlikely any of these girls had the advantages I did growing up in a town with deaf and hearing people who sign. They have found not just refuge here, but a place to grow and learn from one another. Each of these children—with faces like bright flowers—are planting seeds in my mind.

Chapter Thirty-Two

Helene appears, carrying a slate and chalk. She waves her hand toward me to indicate "come."

"Where?" I ask.

I can see from her tight lips and trembling hand that she's agitated as she writes on the slate, *You have shown interest in the teachers and their methods. There is a man who would like to educate us on the matter.*

I slowly nod and wave to my new friends, before returning with Helene to the school.

This must be the private lesson Miss Mitchell mentioned. She's arranging things fast.

Before we enter the building, I reach for the slate and chalk. *Are you going east with the others? You could serve a purpose here. You know the native tongue and are picking up French sign easily and with enthusiasm. I won't go any farther! That wasn't the original bargain. I've been waiting for an opportunity like this. I belong here, and maybe you do too.*

Helene gives me a nervous look and erases my

remarks with her wrist. She writes, *Abbé Sicard arranged this meeting.* I've seen she has doubts about her mission. Will she confide in me?

Miss Mitchell greets us as we enter the building. Her eyes sparkle with excitement.

What exactly is my significance to her? She wouldn't appreciate the comparison, but in a certain way she's like Jack. I want to trust her, but I'm cautious there's a rat trap around the corner.

We enter an empty classroom and take seats—except Helene, who stands by the blackboard with the Interpreter. The instructor arranges his papers. He looks up, thoughtfully examining each of our faces.

I beg you to see into my soul!

As I wish this, I realize the man is the great Laurent Clerc, who Daniel Trees saw in Paris!

He is an imposing figure, with a long face and a lengthy sloped nose. His hairline recedes into smooth white locks. He has a stern look to him, but his demeanor is the opposite. It becomes instantly apparent he must have a strong rapport with his pupils, with whom he speaks freely, hands flying. It's obvious to me we are in the presence of a remarkable person.

I've never seen basic sign taught formally in school. Like everyone in Chilmark, I was taught at home, as a native language is taught to any child. This is what I want to bring home with me! The knowledge of how to teach children with no prior sign language.

Laurent Clerc points to himself and carefully finger-spells his name. He makes the letter *u*—his pointer and middle fingers pressed together on his right cheek and moved downward: his name sign, based on a facial scar.

If the Matron and Miss Mitchell think they are to be given a quick and easy lesson in the signs needed to convert deaf children, I believe they may be in for a surprise, perhaps even an awakening of a nonreligious sort.

Monsieur Clerc looks directly at me as he signs. He's giving me a map of how to teach the deaf who have no natural sign language. I absorb his method and technique. I'm inspired by his presence and passion.

At the same time, I realize I've been learning French sign most readily from the other girls. My conversations with them are invigorating; nuance and shorthand are learned casually, not through formal instruction. So life in the classroom and the dormitory are equally important.

My beloved teacher Massieu told me you inquired about how our French sign has changed since the early days of the school with its founder, Abbé de l'Épée. Let me explain, as I feel you will find it as fascinating as I do. Perhaps you will even relate it to your own island community, of which I knew nothing before your arrival.

I wish I had brought my journal. I'll have to memorize as much as I can, and perhaps Helene will help me fill in the details.

As I'm sure you've been told, Abbé de l'Épée stumbled across two deaf sisters one winter night. L'Épée saw their signs, a natural language of the deaf, as beautiful but primitive. Instead of recording it or studying it, he decided to develop his own unique sign system. It was his goal to re-create the French language in sign language. Borrowing from existing French sign, he created what he called "methodical signs." This approach followed French grammar. I'm sure you can imagine how awkward it was!

I think for a moment, then reply. *It would be akin to converting Martha's Vineyard Sign Language to the exact way people speak English?*

Correct! he signs.

I can tell by their blank expressions that the Matron, Miss Mitchell, and Freckles all feel woefully left out, but I can't waste a moment concerning myself with them. The early attempts at communication that Monsieur Clerc describes, whether failed or not, are crucial to my understanding of deaf languages. I must give him my full attention.

I stand and approach the blackboard. Before Helene can clean it off, I take the chalk and eraser. I need to work it out for myself.

I want apple	becomes	I want **an** apple
Nice meet you	becomes	**It's** nice **to** meet you
Help her?	becomes	**Can you** help her?
Beautiful you	becomes	You **are** beautiful

My hands are moving, trying to turn Vineyard sign sentences into signed English. Not only is it cumbersome, but there aren't signs for the unnecessary words.

He created the "missing" words, which we don't need or use.

As my writing is interpreted for Clerc, he smiles and nods.

Precisely! But please don't judge him harshly. He opened doors for deaf men like Massieu and me. And I believe he gradually changed his mind as he saw our successes.

I nod my head and fist. Never have I felt my calling as a teacher more strongly. Each step in the process is an important one. Do my fidgety companions understand that? Or is their unshakable faith a closed door?

I am not surprised when Miss Mitchell dares to challenge this esteemed deaf man.

Helene writes her speech, somewhat haltingly, and the Interpreter translates in French sign for Monsieur Clerc.

"I don't understand the disagreement. L'Épée's

method makes sense. How else will the deaf write French or English correctly?"

I answer first. *My story in Vineyard sign about the Fisherman touched you. And you know I'm an accomplished writer in English.*

She is thoughtful for a moment. *That is certainly true. I've said you're remarkable. Obviously, Mr. Clerc is too. But I can't imagine how a less than average deaf person, or one who did not have sign language since childhood, learns both and switches easily between them. Why not make them the same, even if it's a bit "awkward"?*

I feel frustrated, but I can also understand her way of thinking. How can I convince her otherwise?

Clerc intervenes. *Mademoiselle, let me tell you my personal story.*

I'm so riveted by his expressive signing that I don't look at the blackboard till he's finished.

My full name is Louis Laurent Marie Clerc. I was born into an important family on December 26, 1785. From the fifteenth century, the males in the Clerc family had served the king through the office of the Royal Commissary.

When I was about a year old, I fell from my high chair

into the kitchen fireplace. My cheek was severely burned, a fever developed. Later, it was discovered my senses of hearing and smell were damaged. I will never know if this accident was the cause, or if my condition was discovered because of it. My parents tried many remedies to restore my hearing. None succeeded. I stayed at home for the next eleven years, taking care of our animals and exploring the village. I did not go to school. I didn't learn to write.

I was twelve years old when my uncle and godfather enrolled me in this school. My age was not a disadvantage. My teacher was my dear Massieu, only twenty-five years old at the time. I learned quickly.

Tomorrow, the two of us will have a public exercise where respectable men and women and members of the general public are free to ask questions. I hope you will join us.

Before he leaves, he turns to me and makes a sign, then finger-spells "liberté." I know that word, and I truly hope it signals my freedom.

Chapter Thirty-Three

"The insolence!" the Matron says, with Helene still interpreting on the blackboard.

"I don't believe he meant it that way," Miss Mitchell replies. I've never before seen her contradict the Matron in front of the group.

I can see the Matron stomp her foot.

Freckles finds her foul voice. "We have been too long in this Popery." More prejudice against Catholics!

"How charitable!" I sign in French. "They are our generous hosts."

They were irate from the asylum's lack of cooperation, but I think they'd be more at home in London than here, where it has become clear some deaf rely less on charity than they first believed.

I was hoping this experience would be as revelatory for them as it is for me. That, when finally faced with a true education for the deaf, they would understand my passion. Especially Miss Mitchell.

A storm is brewing. I can feel it in the tension gathering between us.

A few of the older girls appear in the doorway and look in carefully. When they see that we are no longer under instruction, they beckon with wide grins for me to follow.

"Where?" I ask.

"City," one of them replies, nearly bouncing with anticipation.

When I jump forward, I feel a firm hand clamp down on my shoulder and pull me back. Miss Mitchell stares with steely eyes. She wants to know where I will be. She's not interested, but disappointed.

They're going into the city, I write on her slate. *They want me to come.*

I can see the Matron's haughty laugh and wagging tongue. She doesn't care that I don't understand. They do that purposefully of late, as if to punish me for their shortcomings in learning to sign.

Chaperone, Miss Mitchell writes quickly, and my heart drops as I realize she means herself.

Like a bolt from the blue, I'm hit with inspiration! I point excitedly at Helene, who demurs. But surely, they can see it makes the most sense! Miss Mitchell's mouth is a thin, pressed line, and the Matron's face turns an unsightly purple color. Freckles covers her mouth as her eyes narrow. Her shoulders jerk when she talks.

Helene turns to me with a small smile and nods.

We wear uniform cloaks as we file out the gates in a neat line like ducklings, though we quickly become a messy group. Anne joins me on one side, while her friend Rosalie, with the raven's-wing hair, walks on my other. They chatter to each other excitedly, fingers moving too rapidly for me to catch all of what they are saying. I pick up sweet foods, blue skies, and glorious art.

Helene is at the head, ushering us forward. I'm glad not to be a pupil here, nor the instructor. This is my best chance to absorb the sights!

It's not too far a walk. The cobbles beneath our feet are worn but clean, the sky a sparkling azure. I imagine Paris will be as cluttered as London, but when we arrive, it feels airier. Perhaps it's my mood. I feel lighter with every step.

People pass us but spare only curious glances. I'm sure we make a sight, but the streets are busy with so many more things to look at than a gaggle of deaf girls. It feels good, for once, to be mostly overlooked. A boy holding a stack of papers gives me a concert handbill, which I stuff in my cloak pocket.

Helene writes back and forth with Rosalie, who nods and steers us down a smaller street. The air turns thick with the delicious smells of baking. My mouth waters. The storefronts and stalls are filled with fresh loaves of bread. Their crusts look perfectly crisp. I imagine the insides warm and soft as clouds.

We press our noses like snails against the window of a small shop and then enter in an orderly line. The shelves are piled with the most delicate pastries I've ever seen. We push forward, our feet sweeping the tile floor while we read the smartly written labels.

There are little squares covered in smooth coats of sugar paste, decorated with flowers. Confectionery in different shapes, profiteroles and macarons, filled with jam or cream or coated in chocolate. They all look so elegant. Gazing at them makes me miss Mama's apple tart.

I see the other girls reach for their small purses, pointing to the sweets they want and exchanging a franc or two for them. I feel embarrassed until Anne smiles and buys a sweet for me. I shake my head, but she drops it into my hands.

The profiterole is light as air, its pastry flaky and delicate, the cream within thick and rich. It's arguably the most delicious thing I've ever eaten. Though I mustn't tell Mrs. Pye, who prizes her fish pie with golden crust!

To my surprise, when I glance up, Helene is thanking the shop owner with a hand to her chin that she lowers. Has she become confident in signing? How have I not noticed?

The fingers of our gloves are slightly sticky as we finish our desserts. We wipe them on our cloaks and giggle as we exit.

The street we travel has windows displaying chapeaus with bows as large as the straw hats they rest on, lacy gloves, embroidered tuckers, and purses. Any other day, I would laugh at the assortment of exaggerated finery, but we are all caught up, imagining ourselves adorned in such fanciness. Rosalie raises her shoulder and looks over it coyly as she pretends to fluff a curl beneath her bonnet. She's charming.

I wonder what Mama would do with such a hat, covered in frills and trimmings. It would sit so stylishly upon my head despite my thick, coarse hair.

We linger, drifting apart and together again as we go from storefront to storefront, enthralled by Paris's wares.

Once we have taken our time, Helene gestures to us. She's easy in this role. It's strange, but I am reminded of Chilmark for the first time since I left. Here too we are mixed hearing and deaf. Helene helps and translates for us but makes no big fuss of it. She is simply one of us.

I wonder again if she has ever stepped into a commanding role in which she can be helpful. I think of the bluestockings, a group that advocates for the rights of women. I met two of them at Nancy's house in Quincy last year. I'm sure they would applaud Helene's growing defiance against the league.

When we arrive at the Louvre Palace, I am overcome. It is so grand! I can imagine a king living here. To think that I once thought of the Vale in Waltham, Massachusetts, as the most magnificent building I had ever seen! How sheltered I was. The Louvre—nay, all of Paris!—is a gilded fairy tale come to life on an awe-inspiring scale.

I shake my hands with exhilaration. Helene hands me her slate and I write, *Salon du Louvre.* It is a public museum where all may view some of the most famous artwork in the world. The *Mona Lisa* by Leonardo da Vinci resides here. George was rarely enthused by art, but he spoke of this place with reverence. I will imagine he's gliding along beside me, observing all.

As we enter, Helene warns the girls to behave. They gravely nod in agreement, but I see lots of smiles hidden behind their hands.

The walls are crowded with fine paintings. They're extraordinary even if they don't touch me as Beatrice's drawings did. In the large rooms, they go all the way to the molded ceilings, and we must crane our necks to see. Artists sit with their easels, taking inspiration from their surroundings. I look over the shoulder of one, a young man with a pointed beard. He looks at me, startled, and I sign, "Bon. Good day."

He doesn't understand me, I assume, but he understands the sentiment and takes the compliment with a grin and a nod of his head.

We find *Mona Lisa* in a hallway with red walls. She sits with her hands folded in her lap, her expression enigmatic as she looks out at us from her frame. I tap Anne on the arm, and when she looks at me, I narrow my eyes and try to replicate the painting's mysterious smile.

I see Anne snort, covering her mouth and nose with a hand. When she lowers her arm, she too tries to imitate the subject. A second girl joins in. I give it another go; this time I look sterner, then coy.

I know we're being silly, but when will I have a further chance? I see this outing as an extension of the classroom. I should like to keep my liveliness as I grow, so I don't become a scold again as teacher. Although I miss my students at home, I'd like to teach in a place like the Paris school.

Since I arrived, and have seen what's possible, an idea has been growing inside me like a luminous bubble. Bringing together deaf American youth, including those on the Vineyard where we have our own sign, to a central school where they can grow around other deaf people—policy makers, teachers, friends—would be hugely beneficial. The Paris school isn't just a place where deaf children are happy, educated, and protected by those who understand their challenges and origins—it's the beginning of a deaf country.

A man approaches us with a frown, his finger to his lips. Deaf children truly aren't quiet! I feel Helene's hand on my back, urging me forward. She hides a grin by lowering her head.

When we leave, the sky is turning to evening, the light dim and soft, the color of the world a dusky purple and orange. We must head back. I am tired and happy and ready for rest, so I saunter with the rest of them toward the school.

In a surprise gesture, Helene takes my hand and gives it an affectionate squeeze. I squeeze in return and face her.

"You could stay here and be an interpreter," I finger-spell and sign.

A rosy blush rises in her cheeks. Yet she begins to wilt the closer we get to the dormitories. I think of her walking alone to the visitors' quarters and explaining the events of the day, joylessly, while I bring the sights vividly to life for Little Curls.

Chapter Thirty-Four

A week passes in routine. I wake, dress in my uniform, and have breakfast with my new friends. Classes are about an hour each, with free time in between. I try my best to expand my French sign with history and geography, but drama is my favorite, if only to see Little Curls prance around as she practices for an upcoming play.

The most interesting days are when children of all ages with no formal language arrive from the provinces. Usually unruly, sometimes angry. I watch as they start to see that they are human like anyone else and surrounded by those with similar histories. Maybe not exact mirrors, but a new kind of family.

Sunday is, of course, a day of rest. After Mass, while the others play in the garden, I catch up on all I've done in my journal, until a shadow falls across me.

Miss Mitchell stands beside me and makes the signs for "walk." Just the two of us? She seems good-humored, so I decide to go along, tucking my journal under my arm.

She directs us to a bench, where we sit. She's silent for a moment. Will she press the matter of my traveling beyond Paris? I open my journal and place the pen and ink between us. *Do you have a beau back home, Mary?* she writes.

The question throws me off guard. *No*, I answer. I consider it for a moment before expanding, *I suppose I've been driven by my own wants and interests.*

She nods.

Do you? I write. I'm being cheeky and ignoring the proprieties that go along with the difference in our ages and position.

Her lopsided smile spreads up onto one cheek as she shakes her head, then pauses to observe the garden.

I think we're the same, she writes. *We are both young women of passion, who will do what we need to manifest the things we want. That is oftentimes not understood by others.* She looks me in the eye. *But we understand each other.*

I meet her gaze steadily. *I'm not sure I even really know you*, I write.

She throws her head back and laughs. Have I shocked her with my boldness?

Perhaps, she writes. *Perhaps you know me too well when you look in the mirror. Remarkable women always have to fight harder than others, don't you think? I do. I fought for this journey.*

Why is she imploring me to see that our goals are the same when the past months have proved anything but?

Later, we crowd into a large hall, filled with citizens of Paris curious about this unique school in the heart of their city.

From what I understand, while two hearing men—Abbé de l'Épée and Abbé Sicard—are responsible for the creation and operation of this institution, their deaf students, Jean Massieu and Laurent Clerc, are the proof of its success. They captivate people near and far, who have never met anyone like them.

My traveling party—which now includes the seven additional young women from the American League of Commissioners for Foreign Missions who have joined the holy relics—is delighted by this exhibition.

Everyone around me appears equally thrilled, but I feel suspicion arise in me. Today's performance has been arranged to create a spectacle, with deaf men as the fantastic attraction. At the same time, they are brilliant and also capable of choosing to take part. I'm both proud of them and dreading what the public will ask. I like Parisians, but I don't imagine they're free from bigotry.

At the last moment, Helene squeezes in next to me. An orator at the front will interpret the men's French sign language into spoken French. I'll try to follow their signs. But it's good to have Helene's help if I need it.

I feel a gentle tap on my shoulder and turn to see Miss Mitchell sitting behind me. She looks as serene and friendly as the first day we met. What's her game? I'm not a bird in a cage, nor a falcon with leather straps on my legs to keep me from flying away.

The lights brighten in the hall. The orator warms up the crowd before the audience's questions are put to Massieu and Clerc. Helene winces before translating his message.

Ladies and gentlemen, there exists no longer between the Deaf and Dumb and those who hear and speak that barrier which separated them for many centuries, and which a charitable philanthropist of France has had the courage and talent to overcome.

How painful, how difficult, were the first essays of the inventor! Deprived of all assistance in a career full of difficulties, he flattered himself he should be able to teach a language, by means of the grammar of that language, without reflecting that an idiom, the words and syntax of which are unknown, cannot be taught without the aid of a tongue with which it may be compared.

How then, you will ask, did the inventor surmount the obstacles which were incessantly opposing . . . ?

Abbé de l'Épée is understandably much revered, as he created this foundation. But he is certainly being puffed up! Either the translation is awkward, or the language is florid. Helene shakes her sore wrist, and I indicate I don't need to know the rest of the speech. My Chilmark nature cannot abide too much prattle. Helene writes again when he comes to the point.

> *The men whom I am about to introduce to you will, I trust, furnish a satisfactory proof of the inventor's successes.*

He introduces Jean Massieu and Laurent Clerc. I notice they receive an ovation. And there are several deaf students, leaning against the walls, who wave their hands over their heads—like my deaf applause, seen, not heard. I join them for a quick moment.

The first distinguished woman asks a question that amuses the audience. Helene writes it for me.

> *Question: Would you have any objection to marrying an English lady?*
> *Laurent Clerc: As much an English as a French lady.*
> *Q: Why so?*
> *LC: Because I am not rich enough to support both her and our children.*

There is cheering again. For what? A frivolous exchange. His humor is amusing. But one might ask Monsieur Clerc anything about sign language and the deaf culture he's helping to foster.

The next inquiry is for Massieu and has more substance.

> Q: *What is your definition of hope?*
> *Jean Massieu: Hope is the flower of happiness.*

Clerc also defines the term.

> *LC: Hope is the expectation of a happy event.*
> *Q: What difference do you believe may exist between noise and sound?*
> *JM: Noise is the effect of several objects clashing one against another, by which the surrounding air is struck, and causes a disagreeable sensation to the ear of the hearers-speakers. Sound, on the contrary, strikes the ear without violence or confusion.*

Thinking about these exchanges, I'm reminded of

something I understood while attempting to give Beatrice instruction in her filthy cage at the Vale. What did I write in my journals? *It occurs to me that an apology is harder to convey than pointing to things and naming them. Still, there's no reason any deaf person can't learn to express the full range of emotions.*

That's what's happening here. The audience of "hearers-speakers" (I *will* use this term) wants to be convinced that these learned deaf men can understand abstract ideas rather than just giving objects names. This is deeply insulting—even demeaning. Was I naive in hoping to learn Massieu's story?

I recognize these questions may have to be answered a million times over before we achieve true equality. Massieu and Clerc know this. Their pride is not compromised by their passion for teaching. Can I humbly follow their example? I hope it won't be necessary for deaf Americans to perform publicly to make people understand we're equal. From the ruckus I've observed in the Chilmark Meeting House, I can't see that going well!

Chapter Thirty-Five

I'm to stay in the visitors' quarters until we leave. I don't know who Miss Mitchell talked into assisting her, or how she communicated her demands, but when she invites me back for prayers and to introduce me to the new young missionaries who have arrived, I spy my trunk in an adjoining room. They have been staying in a grand suite, more suited for one of Napoleon's dignitaries. What a compromise it must be for the relics to be treated like nobility!

I thought I was safe here with so many deaf people. But now I'm isolated again among hearing people who don't know my language and have designs on my future that are not my own. I feel a heat rise within me as I watch the new missionaries describe their voyage in spoken language, as if we were not in this place and I were not present. They obey the Matron and fawn over Miss Mitchell.

I notice Helene sits alone with eyes lowered. Can I

appeal to her for help before the Matron's plan is in motion?

She will not meet my gaze.

My heart races. The Matron makes some sort of rousing speech. Miss Mitchell rises, her eyes flashing with the same bewitching look that entranced me in Tisbury. She signs: "help," "save," "eat," "walk," "follow."

Is that how she sees the instructors and students at this school, as helpless, compliant elephants?

My hands start to shake. I slowly approach her. Her lopsided smile looks smug, even sinister.

She tried to convince me that we're the same—ambitious young women working toward a good cause. The writer on our voyage warned me of being put on a pedestal.

I blink away crimson, seeing Miss Mitchell clearly for the first time. She tried to keep me doubtful and trailing behind her to serve her purpose, never *our* objective.

I steady my hands and politely ask questions in my journal. *Such simple words you signed. Are you forgetting the story of Clerc's youth or the sign grammar that Massieu explained?*

She blushes but looks pleased that I'm asking her opinion. Does she not notice my growing resentment?

She writes, *I will never forget the majestic bearing of Clerc and the unfortunate circumstances he's risen above to occupy such a position. As for Massieu, I think Abbé de l'Épée's methodical signs suit our purposes best. We will use French letters and signs but with English grammar that we all know. Helene has been using the skill Our Lord gave her to create drawings of the alphabet and other signs.*

I turn to Helene, who still won't meet my gaze.

I reply. *I'm glad we share an admiration for Laurent Clerc. I hope that if your converts branch away from your original method, like Abbé Sicard did with Abbé de l'Épée, you will follow their lead.*

Miss Mitchell reads my reply aloud and the new missionaries who haven't met me seem impressed by my aptitude. Crimson sparks, like small flames, flash in the room. I will not be plunged back into my terrifying visions. If I can't convince her of Clerc's and Massieu's methods, I can at least make it clear I will not be party to them.

I make the sign for "water." Helene finally rises and places a glass in my hands. I pretend to drink.

Miss Mitchell writes in my journal again. I dread what she's written even before I read it.

I will have you with me, my dear friend. To keep teaching me and reaching out to those who can only aspire to your achievement and faith.

They mean to kidnap me, just as Beatrice warned. Her fear for me has become reality. I am afraid for myself. They have decided for me, I am their tool. Years I could be gone, Mama and Papa worrying over me, never knowing.

I shake my head. Reverend Lee would be horrified by this betrayal. I remember Psalm 36:3 and write openly in my journal. *The words of their mouths are wicked and deceitful; they fail to act wisely or do good.*

Miss Mitchell's eyes dart away. Is she so sure of her command over me?

The Matron brings out a Bible I've not seen before, a grander version of the one the league carries for study. It is marked with favorite passages, as is mine. She quickly skips over the scriptures to the inside back cover, where columns of names are written in different hands. My family and others record births, marriages, and deaths on these pages.

When she lays it out on a table, I realize she's going to have us all sign. It's a contract for a bigger commitment I have no intention of making. Can they force me?

The other girls line up and, one by one, say a prayer before writing their names and joining the others.

When it is Helene's turn, she lifts the pen, then puts it down!

Freckles approaches her and pulls the locket out from under her neck scarf. She gently unclasps it, causing Helene's knees to buckle as she stares at the photos inside. I cannot see anything, but I assume they lost their parents at an early age.

Should I make a commotion to break the spell?

Before I can, Helene signs her name in the Bible. My heart sinks. But I understand the bond between siblings and the devastation of early loss. I can forgive her. In fact, there's nothing to forgive.

Helene uses French sign language to try to draw me forward, imploring me, I think, to add my name to the list. But when she lowers her hand, she spells "run"!

Before anyone notices, I slip to the back of the room. But when I try the door lever, it won't budge.

I look back to find Miss Mitchell watching me with an evil gleam in her eye.

"Open it!" I command. The sign is obvious, like turning a key.

She simply looks away and talks to a scrawny girl in a short gown and worn bonnet.

I stomp over to the Matron, point at the door, and again make the sign for turning a key. Helene is doing her best not to engage with me, and Freckles seems to be shielding her from my influence. Everyone is aware of my ire, but tactfully ignoring me.

I glance at the light in the oil lamps and wish I could ingest the heat and flame and breathe it out like a fiery beast.

I grab a lamp from the nearest table, careful not to tip it. The flame flickers in the glass bulb, but the oil keeps it burning as I move hastily. Shoving it onto the sill, I throw back the drapes and turn the lamp's knob, opening the wick more fully. The fire within flares, reaching above the frosted globe, singeing it with black smoke and licking at the damask curtain.

The Matron rushes to drench the curtain with a glass of water before it's engulfed. Helene finally comes to my side and gently takes the lamp from my hands. I bang my fist on a windowpane.

Miss Mitchell's face looks like a broken theater mask, neither comic nor tragic. She's careful to turn her back to the others so they don't witness her ire.

"Stop!" she signs repeatedly. She remembers that word.

I rush to the door and aggressively shake the latch, knowing no one outside is likely to hear. For a moment, Helene seems to be pleading with Miss Mitchell to let me go—even kneeling down to pray. That finally catches the attention of the group.

Miss Mitchell nods at them courteously as Freckles pulls Helene's arm to make her stand.

Miss Mitchell drags me out of the room, binding my arms with hers. What does she intend to do with me? Throw me into the Seine? Rally sympathy to her side?

I am wondering why she quickly lets me go when I spy Jean Massieu stepping out of the shadows. She must have heard his footfall. How long has he been waiting there? He carries a chain of keys and beckons me to follow him. I don't know what doors he has access to, but I feel the anger go out of me. I almost collapse before he takes my arm.

I can't help but look over my shoulder. Miss Mitchell watches us leave, the mask of her face reassembled, the sweet, lopsided smile back in place. She may be a hearer-speaker who belongs to a league, but the deaf are slowly becoming a nation, and she's put herself outside our borders.

Chapter Thirty-Six

Massieu and I exit the building and cross the campus under the light of a full moon. We don't sign yet. He understands I was in danger, and I'm shaken.

We enter a building and climb a flight of stairs to his office. The room is cramped but comfortable and filled with gathered objects: stones, feathers, and an abandoned wasp's nest. He removes a pile of books to find me a chair.

I thank him for helping me. He shakes his head, indicating he doesn't want praise. He takes a bite of a stale baguette on his desk, then rips off a piece and offers it to me, but I demur.

His signing is very expressive. He chats animatedly; a handful of signs and the shake of his head tell a whole story. Our shared understanding becomes intimate and comical. I learn that he and others at the school were willing to give the missionaries a chance until they saw how the league was using me. With just a glance or wave, he imitates each of the relics—how rude and unaccommodating they have appeared to the school's inhabitants. Then he points at me, his eyebrows raised in a question.

What should I tell him? Practical matters first. "I need my trunk. They have it."

He scribbles a note before opening the door and stamping his foot. I can feel the vibrations as a boy comes running. Massieu gives him the message and returns to his seat.

My attention is drawn to a primitive painting behind his desk. Nothing like Beatrice's drawings or the artwork at the Louvre. When I point to it, he removes it from the wall and blows off the dust, staring at it for a moment with a sentimental smile before passing it to me.

Heavens! Are those sheep in a pasture with a little farmhouse in the back? There's a blue streak that could be a stream or a pool. And bright sunflowers. Two children are playing in front. I know this place—we both know it.

I put my hand palm down next to my leg and raise it up—then point to the painting. I'm asking him if he grew up there. He looks at me curiously. "I grew up there," I sign.

I make the Vineyard sign for "sheep," holding an animal between my two hands, then shearing its sides. He laughs and shows me his sign, like clippers snipping up your arm.

"You, teacher," he signs.

I don't know how to answer. I'd like to be. I hope I am. Every fiber in my being has been reinvigorated by what I've seen at this school. I'm keenly focused on how I may be of use and give my life purpose. I will assist in creating such an institution on our shores and turn away no one, if it's up to me.

"Need learn more," I sign.

He makes the French sign for "ocean," which is like the Vineyard sign. He indicates swimming a great distance.

I stare at him, and he laughs. I laugh too. "No, boat, long voyage," I sign. What is he telling me?

"I came a long way to learn from teachers like Laurent Clerc and you," I sign. "To see for myself if there is a place like this."

I don't think that's what he was asking. "Will I

travel back home? Maybe. I haven't figured out my passage yet. I have students back home. Chilmark. Island. America."

He nods, satisfied.

"You and me, swim back, together?" I tease.

We both laugh.

"Clerc would like to go to America," he signs. Wouldn't that be something!

I pick up the painting again. It makes me miss home, especially when I realize I haven't responded to Mama's letter yet.

The two little figures reach far back inside me. Halcyon days with George, preserved in memories like flowers pressed in a book. Fading, but touching and real.

"You have brother?" I ask. I don't remember the French sign for "brother," so it's more like "boy like you." I think he understands.

He makes the sign for many children. A big family.

"Tell me," I sign. "Please."

He seems gratified to be asked his story. He rubs his chin.

"Tomorrow, my class, you teach," he signs. Does he

believe I'm capable? I am honored and feel truly accepted here.

"Scared," I sign, shaking my hands and biting my lip.

"No," he signs. "Little lesson you teach. You tell about your home. Then I tell my life and they ask questions."

Oh no, not one of those audiences! But he nods and then gestures for me to follow him. He'll escort me to my own quarters. Instead of returning to the dormitory, I am given a room of my own. My trunk is already there.

Before he leaves, he puts his hands together, reminding me to say my prayers.

"Tomorrow morning, nine. Remember," he signs.

How could I forget?

When I open my trunk, I discover that some of my clothes are gone. I won't miss them, but they shouldn't have been taken. Freckles is near the same size as me, and it is conspicuous that the nicer things I sneaked in with the dowdy attire are missing. At least Papa's leather satchel is there. And my journal—which looks as though it has been leafed through. Now they know what I think of them. Mama's letter fell out, but I have it.

Will the missionaries depart without saying goodbye? I desire to see Helene one more time. I don't want the commotion I made in their chambers to be our last memory of each other.

Liberté—what does it mean to me? Is that what I truly desire? How will I ever get home?

I suddenly recall that Mama mentioned Daniel Trees is docking his ship of goods in France for several weeks and will visit Paris. Perhaps he is still here.

I don't have the strength to prepare a lecture for the morning, so I'll have to improvise. But first I write to Mama and shall give it to Massieu to send posthaste.

Dear Mama,

I am glad to hear that Nora is getting along so well, even if she is proving a poor replacement for my bumbling at the chores.

I have no doubt she'll find a place among the island folk.

Please tell Liam I am impressed with how he is

coming along. And I am heartened to hear that Yellow Leg hasn't changed.

Things haven't gone exactly as planned. (When do they ever?)

But I'm learning so much at the deaf school in Paris, and it's what I've been looking for.

To bring this way of education—in sign language, with deaf teachers—to America would be even greater. Though we have an established sign language on the Vineyard and perhaps in other parts of the country, I believe it would be most exciting to mix deaf people from our land, each learning from one another.

I look forward to seeing your garden. Please don't worry about me and miss me too much. I know that's asking a lot. But I carry you and Papa and the best of Chilmark with me at all times.

As a matter of fact, I've been invited to give a small lecture tomorrow morning and I can think of no better subject.

I intend to locate Daniel Trees very soon. I know you're waiting for word of me and my return. One may come soon and the other may be delayed.

I don't know my mind yet.

Yours always,
Mary

I don't tell her I got involved with intrigue in London. Some stories are better shared in person. I hope Massieu can locate Daniel Trees in Paris so he can bring the letter when he returns to the Vineyard. I tuck the envelope under my pillow. Sleep comes as swiftly as the feather that loosens itself from my pillow and glides to the floor.

Chapter Thirty-Seven

When I arrive in the classroom, fear gets the better of me. Have they all come to watch me fall on my face?!

Little Curls, Anne, Rosalie, and the rest of the girls' dormitory, along with several boys I haven't met, watch me closely. Some teachers stand at the back of the room. Massieu sits at a child's desk, his long legs tucked up against his chest. I've dressed in my simple frock, which still smells faintly of salt water from Mashpee.

Massieu's smile gives me confidence. So does the Interpreter. She will translate into written French what I write on the blackboard in English.

I sign and finger-spell mostly in French sign language as I try to paint a vivid picture of my island. Vineyard sign keeps slipping in. Especially our unique Chilmark signs or my family's shorthand, which I've never been so keenly aware of before. I keep telling myself there isn't one right way. The idea is to learn from one another—and spread goodwill.

"I don't know how many of you have ever lived on an island, but almost everywhere you go, you can see the ocean. Though I must walk on land, I think I prefer the water.

"In many ways, my village lives by the tides. Not only do they change the depth of the water and the position of the shoreline, but they determine what boats go out and come in that day. The best time to fish is when the tide is 'running'—that means, it is on the move from high to low or the other way around."

I can feel the raptness of my audience. I pause, trying to think of something I can tell them about our unique deaf community that they may not know.

"There are hills on the island, and my neighbors sign to each other using their spyglasses! One person watches the other start the conversation. Then they put down the small telescope and respond as the other party peers at them. Villagers express their love or argue this way."

I can see the audience laugh. I'm inspired by Mama's story about Nora.

"Hearers-speakers sometimes sign to each other

when no deaf people are there. This is usually when they are sharing gossip or an impolite story they don't want to speak aloud. For example, if they're remarking on a neighbor who hasn't bathed for a month, and everyone smells him coming!"

There's more hilarity in the hall.

One of the girls raises her hand. I point to her. "Are you allowed to go to school there?"

"Yes, of course," I tell her. "As a matter of fact, I was the town schoolteacher before I left."

Anne asks, blinking back tears, "Did you have a time early in your life when no one could understand you and they looked down on you?"

"No," I sign gently. "My papa was deaf, and Mama and my brother George knew Vineyard sign language. I was not seen as inferior until I was kidnapped at eleven years old."

This sends a curious thrill through the crowd as questions fly around me. "That's a story for another day," I say evenly. "Let's just say you oughtn't chase a stranger you've deemed a rogue across a beach throwing pebbles. Be cautious among those who think us inferior."

I can see they're measuring my experiences against their own. Of course, each of us has taken a different path to be in this room. I've realized there are many ways to be deaf.

"So many people in your town are deaf—but why not everyone?"

"No one can figure that out. Papa and I are deaf. A high percentage of us are born completely deaf without any other anomalies. Boys and girls alike. Are your families the same—some deaf and some hearing? Do any of you use sign language at home?" A couple lift their hands, but most just look down.

I sign thoughtfully, "Perhaps not at the same rate as Chilmark. None of us know why. I don't think the *why* is as important as *what* we do about it. We all must achieve liberté, as I have found here!"

Silent clapping goes around the room till everyone is standing. Flustered, I gesture for them to sit.

Little Curls decides to tease me. "My maman told me your President Washington chopped down a cherry tree!"

"That's a popular legend," I sign. "It's said, when he was six years old, he was playing with a hatchet and damaged his father's cherry tree. When his father discovered what he'd done, he became angry. Young George said, 'I cannot tell a lie,' proving his virtue."

I wink at Little Curls and add, "To tell you the truth, I've never believed that story myself! But I certainly enjoy cherry pie."

Rosalie is sly. "What was it like traveling with those sour ladies?"

"Let's just say I caught up on my writing."

"Do you ride buffalo and eat bark from trees?" a boy asks me.

"Such notions about Americans!" I reply with mock outrage. "You have my promise I've never ridden a bison. Some do make a medicine from willow bark, for headache and back pain, but we have a regular diet of corn, cod, lobster. Anything Mama can grow and the catch of the day from the local fishermen."

Now many hands are raised in the air, presumably with similarly preposterous questions.

Massieu comes to stand next to me. I take a seat up front. I think of the painting in his office with the two boys and our different signs for "sheep." I sign, "Will you please tell me your story?" He hesitates only for a moment. However many times he's recited it, it feels fresh and his audience is spellbound.

"I was born in the Cadillac district in the Gironde. My father died in 1792 and my mother is still alive. In our family there were six deaf-mutes—three boys and three girls. The oldest boy died.

"Until I was thirteen years and nine months old, I never received any kind of education. I was unschooled. I told my ideas using manual signs or gestures, which are different from those of educated deaf-mutes. Strangers did not understand when my family used such signs, but our neighbors did.

"I saw many cows, horses, jackasses, pigs, dogs, cats, houses, vineyards, and vegetables growing in open fields. Seeing these things, I remembered them well.

"As I said, when I was a child, I couldn't read and write. I watched other girls and boys going to school and felt jealous. With tears in my eyes, I asked for permission to go. I picked up a book and opened it upside down, showing my stupidity. I put it under my arm as if to pretend I was going off to school. My father would not let me go. He signed to me that I could never learn anything, for I was deaf-mute. This made me cry for many nights, but I was not discouraged.

"No children my age would play with me. They looked down on me. They thought I was like a dog. I passed my time alone playing with a spinning top or a mallet and ball or walking on stilts.

"Sometimes my parents had me look after their flock of sheep. And sometimes people who passed pitied me and gave me a little money. One gentleman took a liking to me and invited me to his house to eat and drink. Later, when he traveled to Bordeaux, he told Abbé Sicard about me. Abbé Sicard offered to begin my education.

"I began my studies by tracing the letters of the alphabet. Several days later, I could write a few words. Within three months, I knew how to write many words; in six months, I could craft sentences. In one year's time, I wrote pretty well. As more months passed, my writing improved, and I could give good answers to a few questions. I had been with Abbé Sicard for three and a half years when we came together to Paris. In four years, I had become as well-versed in many things as people who hear and speak."

I am enraptured, as is the rest of the audience. We all rise in silent applause until Massieu gestures to the back of the room. Abbé Sicard has joined us. I realize he is going to put questions to Massieu. For the students' benefit or mine?

>AS: *My dear Massieu, before you were educated, what did you think about people who moved their lips in the presence of one another?*
>JM: *I thought they were expressing ideas.*
>AS: *Why did you think that?*
>JM: *Because I remembered a time when someone spoke to my father about me and then afterward, he threatened to punish me.*

Before I can process this story, Sicard continues.

>AS: *What is gratitude?*
>JM: *It is the memory of the heart.*

I hardly have time to absorb what an exquisite reply that is before Sicard is on to the next question.

> AS: Did you pray with ideas, words, or feelings?
>
> JM: My heart prayed. I did not yet understand words or their meanings.
>
> AS: How did your heart feel?
>
> JM: Happy when I saw the plants and fruits growing. Sad when they were ruined by hailstorms and when my sick relatives did not get well.
>
> AS: Did you know who had made a cow or horse or other animals?
>
> JM: No, but I was very curious to see birth. I often hid in a ditch where I could see the sky meet the earth and make things grow. I wanted very much to see it.
>
> AS: Did you imagine the sky had a shape or form?
>
> JM: Once my father showed me a large statue in the church near our home. It was of an old man with a very long beard, and in his hands, he was holding a globe. I thought he lived above the sun.

> AS: What did you think when Abbé Sicard first made you trace words with the letters of the alphabet?
>
> JM: I thought the words represented the objects I saw around me. I liked the way they looked on the page. I memorized them with great enthusiasm.

The two men pause. Are we finally done?

Abbé Sicard strides to the front of the room and takes his place at Massieu's side. Teacher and pupil, now also a teacher. I can't help but feel there's vanity in Sicard—the way he wanted Massieu to tell tales of his great success. But whose success was he flaunting, Massieu's or his own? Can hearers-speakers help the deaf without requiring applause?

But, of course, it happens all the time on the Vineyard! Where would I be without Nancy, listening at keyholes and sharing her findings with me when we were children?

It strikes me that an ideal would be to spread the model of the Paris school—deaf children brought here from everywhere to learn and play together.

And, at the same time, to have communities where the hearing are adaptable to deafness and signing—so children like the young Massieu and Clerc, my friend Anne and my dear Beatrice, do not have to endure pain, isolation, and abuse before finding acceptance and achievement. And girls like my younger self cannot be stolen away into a hostile outside world.

I don't know if any of this is possible, but I'd like to think it is. I once asked Papa, if deaf children from the Vineyard went to a school like this, would we lose our Chilmark identity? He didn't seem to think so—but I'm not sure. There's a chance that if deaf Vineyarders left the island to attend a safe place on the mainland, they might blend their sign language, marry outside, and not come back. If so, our unique culture could eventually die away.

I can't help but wonder if Beatrice would be welcome at this school. I've met none like her—no Indians nor those who prefer speaking to signing. As these questions flow through me, I realize there are more issues to consider. But my heart remains hopeful and steadfast.

I look up at Massieu, distinguished in his oration and eccentric in his dress. He smiles upon me in a way that makes me believe I can make a difference. I think of the harsh rejection he received as a boy and yet the strength and resilience he showed when he said, "but I was not discouraged." Not to *try* would be the worst thing.

I put my letter to Mama in Massieu's hand. He grasps it and nods his head. I make my sign for "sheep," and he pets the invisible thing tenderly. I understand why he is so beloved.

Chapter Thirty-Eight

I try to hurry across campus, but news of my lecture has spread. Students wave or stop me to introduce themselves. I'm polite but push on. Am I too late?

At the visitors' quarters, I notice the Matron's trunk on the path in front of the building. The relics are well and truly on their way. I release a breath I didn't even know I was holding.

Miss Mitchell appears with a man carrying her box. When she catches sight of me, I see her sigh, her face stern and disappointed. She opens her trunk and takes out the slate and chalk she's wrapped in paper. The paper doesn't catch fire; the air is clear.

She writes, *I didn't think I'd see you again. I hope you will find passage home.*

I begin to sign, then write, *My friend's brother-in-law is here in Paris. He is a sailor and frequently travels from the Vineyard and Boston to Europe and back. He delivered a letter from Mama.*

That's done, then.

I ask, *Is Helene still here? I'd like to have one more word with her.* Miss Mitchell gives me a hard look. A moment passes.

She writes, *Let me see if she's available to meet you.*

I sign that I'll wait, and she goes back inside.

As Helene walks toward me, I observe that her bashful demeanor has returned, but she walks with her shoulders straighter now and looks me in the eye with confidence. I smile gently. Freckles and the Matron are standing behind her, watching me distrustfully.

"Important, you," I sign. "Deaf children, care for. Remember sign language. You help them."

I see her exhale. Her eyes glisten with unshed tears. I fight to restrain my emotions. The two of us making a scene may compromise her position.

My hands and face speak freely to her. "Reverend Lee—who first introduced me to the league—counseled me that hurting those we love is sometimes a natural part of achieving our goals as we grow.

"This weighed heavily on me, and I turned to a wise woman for another opinion. She told me things I did not want to hear, but also understood that I must make my own choices—and mistakes—to learn from them. Do what you must, but remember that, if you go too far out into the waves, you'll get swept under, and it will be hard to reclaim who you once were."

She finger-spells "liberté." We'll carry Paris with us. We quickly embrace before she is called away.

As I'm about to turn around, Miss Mitchell takes up her slate again. *You may be something here, but in the larger world, you're still afflicted.*

It's ugly, but I won't let her words hurt me. I feel deep inside that my journey will take me farther than the missionaries ever could, and that my purpose is truer.

Flustered, I head for the front gates of the school. I'm not in nature—nor near the ocean—where I feel most at home. But walking will help me make sense of things.

I grab my cloak. The early autumn air nips at me, and I'm glad for the cloak's woolen warmth. Slipping my hand into the right pocket, I pull out a crumpled handbill. I forgot I took it when the girls and I explored the city. I smooth it out to see what it's advertising.

Spin me in circles and knock me down! I rub my eyes to make sure I'm not having a vision, or just seeing what I'd like to imagine. But it's right there in print.

My friend Nancy is in Paris! She's performing music at a salon—and I'm holding an entrée for tonight's event. My reflections and plans about where I'll go from here are temporarily put on hold. It's good to have a distraction, and maybe Nancy will offer a solution.

Now I must find something to wear!

I locate Anne and Rosalie and race over to show them the handbill. I point to Nancy's name and link my fingers to say we're close friends. I only remember the French sign for "house," so I finger-spell "home."

They look at each other quizzically for a moment before realizing a girl I grew up with on the Vineyard is also here in Paris. Perhaps it's unbelievable to them too.

I trace my body to sign "dress."

They sweep their hands up and down their bodies. They own nothing more elegant than what they're wearing.

"Teacher?" I'm inquiring if the instructors have finer clothing than what I have.

They look at each other and laugh. Rosalie signs,

"Frock black." She pinches the points of a white collar and indicates buttons down the front. She walks in a circle with her hand on her hip and indicates too loose stockings.

I think it's a fine look for an educator, but not the fancy dress I was looking for.

"Thank you," I sign.

Anne catches my arm gently. "You hear music?"

I push my hands up and down and rhythmically pump air out of my mouth, indicating vibrations. I rub my chest, wiggle my fingers, sign someone playing a piano with me holding on to it, and point to my nose.

Anne views me with utter fascination. "I feel nothing," she signs.

"Try?" I ask.

"I don't remember any music." I'm not surprised because of what she shared of her childhood.

"Try!" I repeat for emphasis, making her smile.

Rosalie is bored and says so. I stifle a laugh. On the Vineyard, we make a small yawn and roll our eyes slightly to signify boredom. The French sign is your index finger twisted on the side of your nose. That's one French sign I won't adopt. I can imagine Liam doubling over, thinking I'm picking my nose!

I guess I'm attending Nancy's concert as I am. I can conceal myself a bit under my cloak. It's no fun if she's not as surprised as I am!

Chapter Thirty-Nine

Nancy's performance, the handbill informs me, will take place in the salon of Madame Deneuve. From what I've picked up around campus, private performances are rarer these days than they were only ten years ago. France's self-proclaimed emperor, Napoleon Bonaparte, continues to censor the arts.

When she realized where I was going, Anne excitedly explained that the salon is the domain of the lady of the house, as is the salon performance. Madame Deneuve is the *salonnière*; it is her home, and she is the hostess of the evening. She had handbills passed out because *salonnières* believe these performances should be shared with the common man—and woman—a space to share ideas, to speak freely among peers and so-called betters.

I am reminded again of the bluestockings in Quincy. I hope these freethinkers are truly welcoming to different people, and are not the hypocrites I found Nancy's companions to be.

Nancy once informed me that Bonaparte dislikes powerful women as much as he enjoys power. He has allowed this tradition to continue but with the role of the hostess diminished to a mistress of ceremonies alone. But I have learned that you can't control the flow of ideas, no matter who you are or how you try.

The handbill also informs me that Nancy will be playing a selection from Haydn's Paris Symphonies, Symphony No. 85, *La Reine*, or "The Queen," to honor Bonaparte's recent marriage to his second wife, Marie Louise. But I feel as if the message is clear: The *salonnière* is still queen!

Rosalie has given me some direction, which gets me mostly to where I'm going. It's a lucky thing I have the handbill because when I lose my way, I can just show it to passersby and wait for them to point the way without words. Street names and numbers make no sense to me.

The cobbles beneath my feet have been worn smooth. The homes that line the lanes I wander are grand, built from rose stone and marble. They have short, well-manicured lawns with small trees shaped into perfect squares. I gawk openly. Nothing here was built before the last century. In class, I learned that modern history in France encompasses the past three hundred years. That is far older than America. What will my fledgling country look like three centuries hence?

When I'm close enough, the manor house reveals itself; lights glow in the windows, and I can see the silhouettes of guests mingling and passing around finger foods. The house itself seems to dance with merriment, the light reflecting in the golden filigree of its accents. I would have noticed it even if it weren't my destination; it is the loveliest among lovely city houses.

The door is open and I push it slightly to enter the foyer. A crystal chandelier twinkles above me; the walls are lined in red velvet. A male servant welcomes me inside, and my cloak is taken by a different servant. I'm underdressed, but no one bats an eyelash.

There are a few fancy guests, with their hair and faces powdered, their clothes made of silk. I'm shocked to see them speaking with visitors in lower dress. Though my keen eyes can spot some condescension on the countenances of the fancy men and women, it is true that discourse between them is free and open.

Most of the guests are more like me, curious and modestly dressed, which allows me to blend in.

The salon is large, with thick brocade curtains draped over every window. The walls are papered in a delicate floral pattern of soft rose, green, and gold. The ceiling is higher than rooms I'm used to and decorated with plaster molding. A golden chandelier hangs from its center.

Chairs have been arranged in a semicircle with an armchair to the side, presumably for Madame Deneuve.

Nancy sits at the forefront, the center of attention, effortlessly balancing a cello. I have watched her enough to know that she is tuning up. The large stringed instrument must make a louder and deeper sound than most because when she first touches the bow to string, I can feel it reverberate within me.

The guests take their seats. I sit to the side, folding my hands in my lap. Nancy is lost in her world of music and thankfully doesn't notice me.

Madame Deneuve is a stately woman with a presence that would be intimidating if not for her personable manner. Her gray hair is powdered and swept into an older style. Her silk gown boasts little rosettes at the neckline. She feels like a lovely curio from another time, before the French Revolution. She commands the room as she spreads her hands to welcome her guests before gesturing to Nancy. I see some polite tittering as she speaks, but of course, it's lost on me.

I'm offered a small crystal glass of spirits. Mama disapproves except when we're ill, or on special occasions like Christmas, but I take a tiny sip and let the sweet taste linger on my tongue. I have heard about the French and their penchant for drink. Ezra Brewer often had a bottle next to his chair—strong homemade brew, nothing like this pleasing bouquet.

The conversation around me seems lively. I smile once or twice when people meet my gaze, but otherwise let my attention drift.

At last, the performance begins. Nancy looks virtuosic as always. I focus on her fingers, how one hand moves along the strings on the neck of the instrument while the other hand glides the bow smoothly across its base. Back and forth, with the graceful flick of her wrist, finding just the right note every time.

Papa often says, "Jack-of-all-trades, master of none." I wonder if my Jack is sightseeing or swindling tonight. The expression doesn't apply to Nancy. She is master of all. From an early age, I've watched her take up any instrument—recorder, harpsichord, fortepiano—and conquer it.

The longer I watch her, the more I begin to see a mouth carved into the center of the instrument, beneath the strings. I know that's what makes the sound resonate. As I sit transfixed, the mouth starts to sing in my imagination, moaning an unearthly tune.

I have been so long uncertain of my situation that the relaxing atmosphere of the salon disarms me. I find my head nodding. At some point, I must drift off in my chair, my chin against my chest, because when I come to, I am looking up into Nancy's surprised face, her hand on my shoulder shaking gently.

"Here, you," she signs. "How?"

"What a fine welcome!" I tease.

She doesn't take the bait. "Really, Mary, I can hardly believe my eyes."

"That expression is a little cliché for you."

This time she's ready. "*What* are you wearing? A gunnysack? I know you're a simple country girl, but it's de trop—too much!"

"A simple country girl, you say! I have been studying with the greatest deaf minds in Paris. Very learned men."

"The school founded by abbots!" Nancy signs. "Uncle told me about it. It sounds fascinating."

At the mention of her uncle Jeremiah Skiffe, I try not to wince or grimace openly.

"Is your uncle here with you?" I ask. "The last time we saw each other . . ."

"He turned tail," she signs, laughing.

I'm incredulous. "He told you?"

"Not exactly. I read between the lines. The girl you were traveling with . . ."

"Her name is Beatrice."

"Right. Did she and her people meet with trouble on our account?"

"I'm glad you asked," I sign. "No, they didn't."

She crosses one elegantly ringed hand over the other and looks deeply into my eyes before breaking her silence. "I thought I might have lost you forever."

"We don't always see eye to eye—but no such luck!"

We embrace and she introduces me to Madame Deneuve and her inner circle. They're colorful and courteous, but I feel my deafness is on display. I may be more conscious of it than ever. When I step away from the crowd, Nancy follows. I don't have to explain to her.

"Let's find a well-lit, secluded couch where we can chat," she suggests, guiding me toward just the spot.

I give her a brief version of my travels. She rolls her eyes at the mention of missionaries and signs, "Oh, Mary, I can't imagine spending two minutes with those devil dodgers!" She never quite grasps that I must take what I'm given and use my wits to navigate. Being hearing, she has advantages in the world that even she doesn't see.

I tell her that Daniel Trees may still have his boat moored in Le Havre, but that I'm unsure what my next step will be. Could I possibly travel with him? He's seen so much! He spoke of the Paris school years ago. Might he know of more places that would enrich me?

"Of course, you'll return with us," she signs.

"Thank you for the offer, but I'm still weighing my options."

"I cannot imagine being the teacher there, with my father watching over your shoulder." Her face is sour.

"It's not just that," I insist. "I miss my students!"

She taps her finger on her lips and looks me up and down. "What are you looking for, Mary?"

"That's a good question!" I don't have an answer ready, so I shift the subject. "Your music was heavenly tonight."

"You couldn't even feel it," she signs, giving me a sideways look.

"Is that what you think?" I sign. "You are stretching all the time, not content with one instrument or composer."

"It's true," she signs. "And you. You're not displeased yet not fulfilled, despite your remarkable alliances at the Paris school."

"You've said it correctly," I tell her.

"How can I help?"

"I'm so glad I found you here, my friend."

"Mary, I hope I always remain in your good graces and privy to your confidences!"

"We've been through so much," I sign. "I can't imagine that will ever change."

"Were you really cast out?" I see her snicker. "I'm a bit jealous of that distinction! Sweet Mary teaching children about paganism."

I shock us both by retorting, "After traveling with the holy relics, I may consider converting."

Nancy throws her head back and changes the subject. "I'm sure your mother wants you back. I've always been envious of your parents. Don't stray too far. Especially after George . . ."

"I must be resolute," I sign. "Don't break me! Stand behind me."

"I'll send Uncle around Paris in the morning to locate Daniel Trees," she signs. "Don't go back to the school tonight. I have a strange foreboding that it's the last time I'll see you, at least for a long while."

Her words strike me deeply, and I agree to her terms.

Chapter Forty

The brocade curtains let in only a slice of sunlight. I awake in a room of tremendous grandeur. Everything at Madame Deneuve's seems high and cold like a vault. A hidden vestige of life before the Revolution. Not to my taste but nevertheless fascinating. More material for my journals, which I hope to edit and see in print one day.

Nancy and I talked till all hours. Sharing memories and secret ambitions for the future. I still haven't set on my next move. I am suddenly reminded of the way I spun around on the beach at Lambert's Cove, when Reverend Lee took me for a visit. I hope my inside compass needle will point me in the right direction.

Nancy comes in with a breakfast tray. I'm glad for the bread and cheese. But a glass of champagne—really?

She reads my look. "Left over from the salon last night."

"A pot of tea?"

"Don't even think about it here!"

"Did your uncle find Mr. Trees?" I inquire.

"Mary, your signing has become odd. I'm struggling to follow along."

I start again, careful not to mix in French sign. "I'm sure going to confuse townsfolk when I get back to Chilmark!"

My friend becomes thoughtful. "Do you think the different sign languages will always stay apart?"

"That's a good question—sorry, I mean question in our sign. No, I think they'll blend."

She considers for a moment. "That can be your grand legacy! Mary, you'll return to America with the French signs, like a bee pollinating flowers."

"I'm glad you think so highly of me!" I sign. "But I'm just a simple writer, a chronicler of tales based on my experiences, and a schoolteacher."

Nancy looks at me askance.

"I'll leave the pollination to someone more suited to the task. But mark my words, the deaf and our languages will converge. There's no other way to achieve equality."

Nancy signs, *"Tricolore! Liberté,* the blue stripe

means freedom. *Egalité*, the white stripe stands for equality. And *fraternité*, the red stripe indicating brotherhood."

"Yes, I have been taught about the French flag." I sign. "Perhaps the deaf will fly our own banner."

Nancy guffaws and bursts the bubble.

"Don't mock me," I sign, without our characteristic teasing. "You haven't met Massieu and Clerc. Wait until the world knows them."

"Why must it always be men?" she laments.

"These deaf men have been unfortunate in their lives and seek to educate others," I sign. "Don't smirk at them." She nods to agree, with some defiance.

"I'll see if Uncle is in his room," she signs before departing.

I open a large wardrobe and rifle through Nancy's clothes for something proper but not too ostentatious. Also, jaunty enough to travel in. I put together a striking outfit. In this new chapter, I want to shed anything to do with the relics.

Chapter Forty-One

Nancy slips into my room unnoticed. She describes a man with broad shoulders, as tall as a tree.

"Daniel Trees!" I sign. His last name is a name sign in my language.

Nancy has a friend of Madame Deneuve's call for a carriage. Fortunately, we ride without Uncle Jeremiah. He's staying in Paris with a musical connection Nancy made back home in Quincy.

"I took some clothes," I tell Nancy.

"They are for sharing at the salon, for those less fortunate who may attend in tatters," she signs, "and it's a great improvement."

"Where are we going?" I sign. "His ship must be moored in the north—near the English Channel. I'd like to see him and give him the letter for Mama."

"Uncle found him lodging at a tavern sailors frequent near the Seine."

"It's been some time since I've seen him," I sign with excitement.

"I don't know if he'll recognize us!" she signs. "We're not little girls anymore."

Daniel Trees is an amazing sight. He's over six feet tall, with long legs and a broad nose. I can see his head is bald beneath his cap. Gold loops adorn his ears. He greets us with his big, toothy smile.

"Hello, girls, I'm happy to see you again," he signs.

I smile because he remembers the signs we taught him when he visited the Vineyard.

He opens his long arms to embrace us. When we were younger, he could carry us both—one under each arm. Nancy demurs. But I run into his warm embrace. In that moment, I'm barefoot and eight years old again, holding George's hand and collecting shells. Daniel Trees brings the island and all its memories back to me. Nancy is doing her best to shake them off.

Why wouldn't I run back home straightaway? That refuge won't always be there or the same.

"You recognize me!" I sign.

"How could I miss that splendid head of hair, bright hazel eyes, and puckish mouth teasing a smile?"

I'm always pleased when someone is fond of my appearance, which I pick at.

"Did you get your ma's letter?" he signs. "She's a fine woman and missing you so."

"I did. Thanks for delivering it to the school."

He cocks his eyebrow. "Do you have a reply for me to bring back?"

I slip it out of my journal and hand it over.

"Just as well," he signs, "I won't be going back there for some time."

I look into Nancy's eyes and recall her portent from last night that we might not meet again soon.

"Where are you headed?" I sign.

"Oh, here and there," he signs.

I hesitate for a moment, then come out with it. "Can I join you on your travels?"

"Young gal, it's not that I don't want you," he signs. "I just don't know if the places I'm going are suitable for one like you."

"I was going to travel to the Middle East and Asia with a league of missionaries," I tell him.

"Why did you change your plans?"

"I had just about enough of their company."

He throws his head back, and his booming laughter echoes.

"I know the type," he signs. "But joining on with me and my mates, now that's something else. What would your ma and da say? Nah, I don't think so."

I must look crestfallen, because he turns to Nancy, who's been standing silent.

"You'll bring Mary back, won't ya? You and your uncle."

Even if it's shorter, making the passage with Jeremiah Skiffe is out of the question.

"I offered," she signs. "But I gather she has other plans."

"Maybe you can stay longer at that deaf school," he suggests. "I'm sure they'd be glad to have you."

"They've been most gracious," I sign. "But I've got something else in mind."

"Well," Daniel Trees signs, "while you think it over, I'll treat you to the best oysters this side of the Atlantic."

Nancy and I agree. I've never had shellfish in Paris, and I've not given up hope of convincing him to take me on.

Chapter Forty-Two

We walk through a raucous part of Paris I haven't yet glimpsed. There's a bar where sailors and tradesmen come to sup, nothing fancy. A waitress brings us a big tray with oysters to shuck, a bucket to toss the shells in, bread and butter, and some ingredients to mix condiments. Nancy and I just sprinkle a little lemon while our host piles on the horseradish.

I slurp the oysters. Cold and briny against my lips, they bring me to my senses.

"I'll have to go back to the school to collect my trunk and say goodbye," I sign.

"I'll take ye," Daniel Trees signs. "Gives me a chance to fiddle with that one-handed alphabet."

"I appreciate your interest in different sign languages," I tell him.

He shakes his head with regret. "It's too bad that Frenchie dictator little Boney stops us from visiting the Iberian Peninsula. Thar's a different kind of sign. Wish you could see it."

"Oh, please take me with you!" I implore. "I promise I won't be any trouble, and I've just got to see more of the deaf world." He rubs his chin while thinking.

"Thar's places you just can't go, Mary. They wouldn't let you in. Take the village on the Mediterranean..."

He slurps down a couple more oysters and chucks the shells in the bucket. I'm on the edge of my seat, but there's no rushing Daniel Trees.

"Both deaf and hearing sign, like your island," he continues. "Here's the kicker. It came from a single extended family with lots of deaf folk."

"Massieu told me his family and their neighbors understood his signs, but nobody else outside."

"I've seen that plenty," he signs. "In this case, it spread to an entire region of the country."

"Are you pulling my leg?" I ask.

"Wouldn't never." He winks and tosses back a brew.

"Do you see why I must travel with you now?" I demand.

"I don't think you'd like Germany much," he signs. "You're not the speaking kind of deaf, and that's all they teach there."

"There must be deaf who at least create their own sign!"

"Haven't met them," he signs. "Those mumbling coves have naught nice to say about the founder of the Paris school. Wrote a book attacking him."

"Attacking Abbé de l'Épée? I take offense at that!"

"Didn't say they were right," Daniel Trees signs.

Nancy delicately wipes her mouth and signs, "I think I'd better be getting on. I told Madame Deneuve I'd bid her adieu before we leave."

"Are you leaving now?" I sign.

"I wish we'd met when I first arrived," Nancy signs. "But Uncle and I can't delay our passage back. You know you're still welcome to join us. I hate to leave you behind. But you seem to have made up your mind."

"I don't know what I'm going to do," I sign. "I am finally free of the missionaries, but my choices are shrinking."

"What did you expect as an American girl on her own in Bonaparte's Paris?" Nancy snips.

Daniel Trees must see me blinking back tears because he steps in.

"Like I said, let's take Mary back to her friends at

the school. They're learned folk and will know what to do. And her belongings are there."

"I honestly don't have time," Nancy signs. "But I'll drop you both on my way to Madame Deneuve's."

Riding in the carriage, I shake my hands in front of me to ask Nancy, "What?"

"You'll never forgive my uncle," she signs. "That's the only reason you're not traveling with us."

"That's not true," I insist.

"Fibber!" she signs. "Do you think he regrets nothing? We all loved George. Uncle can't go back to the Vineyard. He accepts that, and he's tried to help you. I admit he was not always successful . . ."

I sign what I've kept inside. "I still blame myself for the accident." I rub my fist over my heart, like I'm polishing it. "Forgive me."

The defensiveness goes out of her. She signs while looking out the window. "Forget it, Mary."

"Here it is!" Daniel Trees exclaims.

At the front gates of the Paris school, I jump out, suddenly seeing it anew. I've learned and taught here, and now I can take it anywhere. I think I know what I'll do, but I've got to see Massieu one last time.

Chapter Forty-Three

"Can you please wait here?" I ask Nancy. "I have a favor to ask of you and your uncle."

"How long?"

"Thirty minutes at most," I sign.

"I want to pick up a few wares for friends in Quincy," she signs. "I'll visit the shops, then be back here in half an hour. What are you thinking?"

I tell her what I need. She's thoughtful and nods amiably. Daniel Trees and I walk toward the grand institution of learning.

The students wave to me, glad to have me back. Daniel Trees stops to talk to a young man he's met before. I move on, seeking out Jean Massieu in the classroom where we lectured together. Another class is taking place. I pause at the door to watch them.

Yes, it won't be long before we have the same in America.

I remember where Massieu's office is and cross the campus. I run into Little Curls and some of the other girls from my first dormitory.

"Mary!" She caresses the side of her face, remembering Papa's nickname for me.

She and her friends gather around me, examining my new clothes and asking questions. I realize I've been talking with Nancy and Daniel Trees, and my French sign language is a little rusty. But they bring me back into the fold.

"You must come see!"

"We are performing a story."

"I will wear a paper crown."

"I will play an ugly sister."

"I'm a mouse."

"I'm looking for Massieu," I tell them. "I don't have too long, but maybe I can come and find you again."

"Please, mademoiselle! Do not leave us sad."

That I cannot bear to do. "I will try my best to be there."

They depart in a rush of excitement. I stare after them, smiling, memorizing this moment in our lives.

I climb the stairs to Massieu's office and find him looking down at his desk. Perhaps reading or composing a lesson. I will miss his distinct profile, with his hawk's nose. His eyes are penetrating as they meet mine.

"I'm sorry to disturb you," I sign.

He laughs. I repeat the same sentence, remembering my French signs and finger-spelling.

"You are leaving us?"

"I am. I wanted to thank you most of all."

He puts his hand over his heart.

I point at the painting he showed me last time, of the two children with a flock of sheep and a small farmhouse.

"You made me realize I can come from a place similar to your country home and still effect change in the world."

"Teach the deaf children," he signs. "There is no nobler mission."

I nod.

It's obvious that he's busy, so I start to back out the door. His final words are, "Love all."

That's the best I or any other could do. Recalling Miss Mitchell, I know it isn't a simple task.

I am so lost in these thoughts I almost forget I have a performance to attend! I realize I don't know where on this large campus it is taking place. I run into starry-eyed Anne, who asks me about Madame Deneuve.

I answer her questions as she guides me toward the play acting. Before we bid adieu, I ask her to have my trunk sent to the gates. I take her hands and nod my head smilingly. She kisses both my cheeks, Parisienne style.

I recognize the fairy tale as soon as I enter the room. But I've never seen it presented this way.

Little Curls is Cendrillon, or Cinderella. She dons a white robe and gold paper crown. She walks carefully on her tiptoes, like she's wearing glass slippers.

The Fairy Godmother—played by one of the girls who laughed at my signs our first night together—has just prepared her to attend the ball. She holds her head up high, regales us as she signs her enchantments with the wand in her hand.

The mice girls scramble on the floor. They prance with their hands hanging in front of them like little creatures' paws. One makes the others laugh as she pretends to wash herself like an animal. When they are turned into a carriage, they walk nobly, with Little Curls gracefully sweeping the floor in the middle.

It's a magnificent pageant. There isn't a narrator, but every gesture, glance, and toss of the head casts a spell.

I watch as Cinderella is told she must return home before midnight. Oh dear, Nancy and my carriage. I must fly!

I dance awkwardly around the actors, waving goodbye and signing, "Never forget you!" They don't break character, but start sign singing, "Goodbye, Mary, we hate to see you go!" I feel like I'm floating on chiffon, and there are more kisses on the cheeks as they pass by me, the reverie increasing till I'm nearly in tears.

I find Daniel Trees, but he's content to stay in France a bit longer. He picks me up and swings me around. "You've grown up, gal. I trust you to make good choices."

I'm afraid I'll find a cross Nancy at the gates, but her shopping took longer than expected, and she has just returned.

"The crowds of foreigners!" she signs, exasperated. I stifle a giggle.

As our driver races through the streets, I think of Princess Little Curls getting home before the magic disappears. I will forever miss *mes jeunes amies*. I hope they'll remember me for all their days.

Chapter Forty-Four

Uncle Jeremiah is waiting for me and Nancy outside Madame Deneuve's. His grand carriage is filled with luggage. My simple trunk is added to the boot.

"It's very kind of you to do this for me," I tell him.

"No trouble at all," he signs haltingly. "I'm glad to be of service."

There are two seats lined with red velvet, and gold filigree around the windows, the glass smooth and unclouded. We are on our way to the port at Le Havre.

We ride in silence for a few moments before Nancy starts up the conversation once more. "Uncle afforded you the best he could," she signs to me. "His signing is quite awkward now, so I'll tell you."

"Will my passage be the same as yours?" I inquire. "Will my ship be leaving at the same time?"

"No," Nancy tells me, "it departs a couple days after ours. You'll have a private cabin, and the captain has already been informed that you're to be looked after, accommodation needs to be made for communication. You are a young lady of means traveling alone, after all," she says, and sniffs slightly. I hide a grin.

She pauses, and I shake my hands in front of me to ask, "What?"

"It won't be a straight passage, like ours. There'll be a few detours on the way," she tells me, then pauses. I think she looks slightly suspicious for a short while, so I raise my eyebrows at her. She adopts a lecturing posture. "Now, knowing you, don't you go hopping off at a port in Greenland or some such place and start signing with the local population!"

I laugh, but then adopt a serious demeanor. "Well, I can't make any promises . . ."

It's very unladylike, but she throws her handkerchief at me. I stick out my tongue.

When we arrive at Le Havre, men unload the trunks from the boot. They leave my plain wooden one on the side of the cobbled road while they carry Nancy's and her uncle's toward the dock.

"I suppose it's time to say our goodbyes," Nancy says as we face each other.

"Yes," I sign. "But I suppose . . . we've said goodbye before, so we'll say hello again as well." She takes my hand and gives it a gentle squeeze.

"Oh!" I wave my hands, fingers curled into circles. "I've something to ask you." I bend over my trunk and slide my journal out of Papa's leather satchel. I stand and extend the book to her in my hands. It's been well worn, especially these past few months. The pages are bent and fanned; the cover scuffed.

"I've reached the end," I tell her. "There's no more paper left. I suppose I've come to the end of the story within these pages. Will you bring it home for me? I think Mama will be glad of it in my absence, until she sees me again."

"Of course," she says, and takes the journal. "Though I have a small suggestion . . ." She opens the cover and props the book on her knee, reaching for an ink and nib pen. She begins to scribble on the front page.

I try to look over her shoulder and glimpse the words "whereabouts" and "unknown," but she twists to block my view. Her tongue is stuck between her teeth, and she has a mischievous look on her face. I do hope she's not getting me back at Mama's expense!

She stands straight again and nods, satisfied, before tucking the journal away. I'll just have to wait to see what she has wrought. We have one last goodbye, and a rare hug. And then she turns to join Uncle Jeremiah at the dock.

To pass the time, I look for Daniel Trees's vessel, the SS *Atlantic Maiden*. I remember it has blue and green stripes with a small figurehead on the bow of the boat—a red-haired, green-eyed maiden in a blue dress. I imagine she looks marvelous riding the waves.

I sit on my trunk and look out toward the horizon.

I think of the first line of a poem Mrs. Pye had me memorize and recite. I change it a little for my purposes. "The girl stood on the burning deck." There are no flames now, just embers. Remnants of loss and harm I couldn't control. If time doesn't heal all, it keeps us moving along. *If I had stayed at home and only dreamed of here, how much I would have missed!*

Chapter Forty-Five

Adieu,

      City of Lights!

Au revoir,

      Massieu and Clerc!

I'm coming,

      Beatrice and Liam!

But first—

      The sky

    has never looked so wide

      nor the sea

    so deep.

I know my struggles

  were worthwhile,

and I can make use

  of the places

I passed through

   and the people

who passed alongside me.

The world's obstacles—

  town councils,

  missionaries,

hearers-speakers

>   who underestimate me—

> won't be easy to sway. But

>   I won't be alone anymore.

>   I'll drop my anchor

>   in a deaf land.

⌒ HEREDITARY DEAFNESS ON MARTHA'S VINEYARD

From 1740 through the late 1800s, hereditary deafness was common on Martha's Vineyard, especially in the town of Chilmark. Deafness was a recessive trait that affected white settlers equally. The genetic mutation produced complete deafness at birth with no associated anomalies. The population had a unique form of sign language, Martha's Vineyard Sign Language (MVSL), which was spoken by Deaf and hearing residents. When the deaf left the island to attend the American School for the Deaf, MVSL aided the creation of a national sign language—American Sign Language (ASL). As Mary predicts, many lived off-island and did not intermarry, so the deaf population decreased. The last native MVSL speaker, Katie West, died in 1952.

⌒ THOMAS HOPKINS GALLAUDET (1787–1851)

When stories are passed along and become legend, the details sometimes shift. This account of Thomas Hopkins Gallaudet is the most recognized. In 1814, Gallaudet visited his relatives in Hartford, Connecticut. His younger siblings were ignoring another child. When he went to investigate, he discovered the young lady, Alice Cogswell (1805–1830), was deaf. Not knowing sign language, the two found creative ways to communicate.

Watching this progress, Alice's father, Mason Cogswell, financed Gallaudet's trip to Europe to study, as there wasn't a permanent school for the deaf in America.

Gallaudet first traveled to England in 1815. He found the Braidwood family inhospitable. His diary is filled with insults about the school and their methods. American Deaf historian Kathleen Brockway and contemporary British Deaf historians and sign language linguists challenge Gallaudet's account. They say the school did not focus on the oral method of lipreading and speech, but instead used a combined method with British signs. They believe that Gallaudet was offered and rejected the invitation to stay three years to learn the school's methods and how to teach them. He was desperate to return home to open an American school in 1816.

While in England, Gallaudet met Abbé Sicard and two of his faculty members, Jean Massieu and Laurent Clerc. He eagerly followed them back to the Institut Royal des Sourds-Muets in Paris, France. There, Gallaudet learned much but ran out of funds to support himself. Recognizing that he couldn't set up a school on his own, he convinced Laurent Clerc to return to America with him. On the voyage home, Gallaudet taught Clerc English and Clerc taught Gallaudet sign language. Together, they established the American School for the Deaf in Hartford, Connecticut, in 1817.

Gallaudet University—America's only national college for the deaf, which continues to enjoy great renown—was established by Gallaudet's oldest son, Edward Miner Gallaudet.

In this book, I've based much of Mary Lambert's voyage and many of her experiences in England and France directly on Gallaudet's observations in letters and diaries. For example, during his passage to Europe, Gallaudet made friends with the American writer Washington Irving (1783–1859). Gallaudet records the night frights of the author who would write the short story "The Legend of Sleepy Hollow" several years later.

My primary resource is *Life of Thomas Gallaudet, Founder of Deaf-mute Instruction in America*, by his son Edward Miner Gallaudet, Henry Holt and Company, 1888.

IMPORTANT FIGURES IN FRENCH DEAF EDUCATION

Abbé Charles Michel de l'Épée (1712–1789) was a hearing Catholic abbot of Paris who founded the first free education for deaf people in 1755. He learned the signs that were being used by deaf people in Paris and then created his own system. He added a signed version of spoken French. Often referred to as "the Father of the Deaf," l'Épée's influence was enormous, and his method created a boom in the development of international deaf education.

Roch-Ambroise Cucurron Sicard (1742–1822) was a hearing Catholic abbot born in the French provinces. He was principal at a school for the deaf in Bordeaux in 1786, and in 1789, upon the death of Abbé de l'Épée, succeeded him as leader of the Paris school. Sicard wrote several influential essays about educating the deaf. He discovered Jean Massieu as an uneducated deaf boy made to look after his family's sheep and brought him to the Bordeaux school, where he became a great success.

Jean Massieu (1772–1846) was the first Deaf teacher of the Deaf in France. Rescued by Abbé Sicard from a life of language deprivation, Massieu learned to read and write French, and later helped develop the first formalized French Sign Language. He taught at the Paris school for the deaf, where Laurent Clerc was one of his students.

Laurent Clerc (1785–1869) was a French Deaf teacher called "the Apostle of the Deaf in America" and often regarded as the most revered deaf person in American Deaf history. He did not attend the Paris school for the deaf until he was twelve years old, defying the idea that language-deprived children past a certain age cannot be fully educated. He was taught by Abbé Sicard and Jean Massieu. With Thomas Hopkins Gallaudet, he cofounded the first permanent school for the deaf in America in 1817. Clerc's mode of instruction was French Sign Language. His students learned those signs and blended them with their home and village signs. The influence of Clerc's language combined with existing sign languages spread and evolved into American Sign Language (ASL).

Laurent Clerc and Jean Massieu's accounts of their lives and their answers to questions posed to them by Sicard and the public are exact. I translated them from the French text *Recueil des Définitions et Réponses, Les Plus Remarquables de Massieu et Clerc, Sourds-Muets, Aux Diverses Questions Qui Leur Ont Été Faites, Dans Les Séances Publiques, de M. Abbé Sicard, 1815.*

THE AMERICAN BOARD OF COMMISSIONERS FOR FOREIGN MISSIONS

The American Board of Commissioners for Foreign Missions was one of the first American Christian missionary organizations. The Boston-based commissioners were founded in 1810, the year this book takes place. I used it as inspiration for the "holy relics" missionary league. ABCFM believed "the field is the world" and sent male and female missionaries to the Middle East, Asia, and Africa.

In 1817, the Brainerd Mission was opened on a tract on South Chickamauga Creek, near present-day Chattanooga, Tennessee. The mission was intended "to provide a basic education to Cherokee children, while also instilling Christian religious values." The mission was officially closed on October 2, 1838, because of Cherokee removal, a part of the Trail of Tears.

ACKNOWLEDGMENTS

Thanks to Julie Morstad for a third cover art that beautifully portrays Mary's growth and character.

To my knowledgeable and kind agents, Jennie Dunham and Leslie Zampetti, for helping me bring the Show Me a Sign trilogy to a wide audience—may our Mary continue to grow!

My extraordinary editor and dear friend, Tracy Mack—all is possible with you. Thanks for seeing something in my work that no one else did—and for taking this journey with me, Mary, and the rest of the SMAS crew! Special thanks for helping me cross the finish line, when I didn't believe I could.

To Leslie Owusu, who is new to the team, but brought so much creative input, care, and enthusiasm to the project, it feels like she's been on the island since the beginning.

Special thanks to Marijka Kostiw and Melissa Schirmer.

Thank you to the whole team at Scholastic, especially Elisabeth Ferrari, Seale Ballenger, Erin Berger, Lizette Serrano, Emily Heddleson, Sabrina Montenigro, Rachel Feld, Jarad Waxman, Jody Stigliano, Elizabeth Whiting, Jacqueline Rubin, Dan Moser, Nikki Mutch, and Ellie Berger.

It was an honor to receive cultural competence feedback from Black Seminole activist and storyteller Mr. Abe and Deaf historian Kathleen Brockway.

My sister Jean—this book is yours as much as mine.

Thank you to Gabi and the Sheremets, Sabrina and Theresa, AG, Joann with Duffy and Barney, Phillis Filer, Alexis, school buddy Chris Leonardi, and all friends who have shown me patience and given me and my stories support.

⌇The text of this book was set in 12-point Adobe Garamond Pro, a contemporary typeface family based on the roman types of Claude Garamond and the italic types of Robert Granjon.

⌇The title type and author name were hand-lettered by Julie Morstad.

⌇The jacket art was created with pencil and digitally rendered by Julie Morstad.

⌇The book was printed and bound at Grafica Veneta.

⌇Production was overseen by Melissa Schirmer.

⌇Manufacturing was supervised by Katie Wurtzel.

⌇The book was designed by Marijka Kostiw and edited by Tracy Mack.